DEAD

BOONE BRUX

*Enjoy!
Boone Brux*

Dead Spooky © 2016 by Boone Brux

All rights reserved. No portion of this book may be reproduced, stored in a retrieval system, or transmitted in any form or by any means—electronic, mechanical, photocopy, recording, scanning, or other—except for brief quotations in critical reviews or articles, without the prior written permission of the author.

All characters, places, and events in this publication, other than those clearly in the public domain, are fictitious and the product of the author's imagination. Any resemblance to actual persons, living or dead, is purely coincidental.

ISBN: 9781795423526

P.O. Box 211752

Anchorage, AK. 99504

Visit her website at www.boonebrux.com

Other Books by Boone Brux

Grim Reality Series
To Catch Her Death
Styx & Stoned
Fireweed and Brimstone
Dead Jolly

Grim Reality Spinoff
Hellbound in Vegas (Hell to Pay Series)

Wedding Favors Series
Bridesmaid Blues
Random Acts of Marriage
Properly Groomed

Paranormal Romance
Suddenly Beautiful

CHAPTER ONE

I strolled into the living room and stopped beside my mother. "What's up?"

Crossing her arms over her chest, she flicked her head toward the couch. "Your father's dead."

"Bummer." While my gaze traveled over my dad's outstretched body, I lifted my can of soda and took a couple of healthy swallows. Then lowering the can, I said, "You know he's going to start stinking if you leave him there too long."

Mom made a clicking sound with her tongue and rolled her eyes. "He's not really dead, Lisa. He's acting."

I knew dead, and clearly, my dad hadn't kicked the bucket. If he had shuffled off the mortal coil, I would have been delivering his spirit to Hal, my porter. Because I was a grim reaper, death followed me everywhere, meowing like a needy cat, winding around my legs, and tripping me up. If a spirit wasn't on my Must-Reap list, I usually ignored them, but sometimes death wouldn't be denied. It invaded my life like a stinky cat box, demanding to be scooped up and disposed of properly.

But since my parents didn't know about my job at

Grim Reaper Services, I kept that comment to myself. "Are you sure he's not just napping?"

"Of course, I'm sure." A smile creased her mouth, and she looked at me. "He got a part in the community theater's Spooktacular Extravaganza. He's playing a corpse." Returning her focus to my dad, she sighed. "Isn't he wonderful?"

"Mmmkay." Though I didn't think playing the part of a corpse taxed one's ability as an actor, my mom obviously believed dad was pulling off the performance of a lifetime. I grimaced against the look of lusty admiration sparkling in her eyes. "Are you sure you don't mind having the kids tonight?" It was Halloween, and earlier today I'd gotten a call from my boss, Constantine. He had a special assignment for my partner and me, which never boded well for a lot of reasons. Not getting to take the boys trick-or-treating was the least of the inconveniences I was sure to encounter tonight. "They can get kind of wild from all the sugar."

"Of course, I don't mind. We have the whole night planned." She held up her fingers and ticked off the rigid schedule she'd devised for the evening. "First we're getting dressed up in our costumes. I'm going to be a witch."

"Fitting," I said.

"Then—" Her voice increased a few decibels, trying to drown me out. "We're trick-or-treating downtown for an hour. That gives us just enough time to get to the theater for the Spooktacular Extravaganza. It's going to be so much fun, the boys probably won't even miss you."

"Of course, they'll miss me." I bristled at my mom's backhanded comment. "I'm their mother."

"Of course, you're their mother, but I'm grandma." She straightened and folded her hands in front of her stomach. The pose was what I referred to as her victory stance. Anytime she thought she'd out argued somebody, she struck that pose. "Grandma's are always more fun than moms."

"Mine certainly was," I mumbled, giving her a tight smile, deciding the subject of who was more fun was not worth arguing over—because clearly, it was me. "Anyway, thanks again. Bronte is staying at Fang's house tonight, but she knows to call here if she needs anything."

"Fang." A curt snort ejected from my mom. "What kind of name is that?"

"Hmong, she's from Vietnam." My daughter's best friend was a tiny Asian girl, who had embraced the American culture after moving here from Vietnam. With Fang's overbearing mother and sixteen siblings, I felt confident this year Bronte wouldn't get into much trouble. If she did, I'd know about it within ten minutes. "I'm going to say goodbye to the boys." I leaned in and gave her a kiss on the cheek. "I'll call tomorrow morning before I pick them up."

"Okay, honey." The look on her face made me pause as if she knew something I didn't. "Don't work too hard."

"I won't." I stopped. "Are you sure you're okay with this?"

"Go." She pointed toward the door. "We'll be fine."

After a few more seconds of scrutinizing her, I pushed away my suspicion that something was up and looked at the brown floral couch where my dad still laid. The corner of his lip quivered as he exhaled, and I was pretty sure he'd fallen asleep. Yeah, he was a true professional. "Tell dad to break a leg when he wakes up."

"He's acting, not asleep," my mom called after me.

"Well then, tell him to break a leg after he stops acting like he's asleep." I stopped in the foyer. "Boys, come give me a hug."

Thunder created by four little feet pounded up the stairs from the basement game room. The twins rounded the corner, slid across the wooden floor in their socks, and barreled into my open arms. I loved my boys. They'd kept me sane after my husband died, and they made me laugh with their shenanigans. But were they ever a handful at times.

"Why can't you take us trick-or-treating, Mom." Breck squeezed my waist, blocking off most of my oxygen intake.

"I'm sorry, honey, I have to work." I pried his arms from around my waist and knelt. "But grandma and grandpa are going to make sure you have a great time."

Bryce wrinkled his nose and dropped his voice to a whisper. "Grandma smells like bologna and she's always hugging us."

"She hugs you because she loves you." I leaned toward them and matched his whisper. "And she smells like bologna because of the preservatives. That's what holds her together and stops her from turning into a mummy."

Their eyes widened. "Really?" they asked in unison.

"Oh, yeah." I nodded and stood. "Otherwise..." Extending my arms in front of me, I moaned, doing my best mummy impersonation. "Brains. I want brains."

"Mummies don't eat brains," Bryce scowled.

"Yeah, Mom." Breck shook his head. "That's a

zombie."

Okay, so my impression wasn't good. Like I'd admit that to them. Lowering my arms, I glared at them with my best, *you're dumb* look. "I know that. Grandma is a zombie mummy. Duh, shows how much you guys know."

"She is not." Bryce crossed his arms over his chest and gave me a skeptical glower. "There's no such thing as zombie mummies."

"Whatever you say." After grabbing my purse off the hook I turned back to them, staring for several exaggerated seconds. "But…you might want to make sure grandma eats a bologna sandwich before bed. You know, so you don't wake up to her trying to snack on your brains." Both of their mouths sagged open, which was highly satisfying for me. I smiled and then chirped, "Bye."

With that, I opened the door and headed into the crisp October afternoon, the boys' conspiratorial plans whispering after me. It was a little cruel to tease them and even crueler for my mom, but all of them gave as good as they got. Actually, they usually gave tons more than they got. A chuckle rumbled from me. I hoped my mom liked bologna sandwiches. I was fairly certain that's what the boys would be requesting for dinner—and a before-bed snack—and would be on her nightstand in the morning.

It was one o'clock when I pulled into the GRS parking lot. I parked my new black Ford Explorer next to Nate's Suburban. I'd like to say I missed my old van, Omar, but I didn't. Not even a little. My sleek black SUV totally mirrored the badass grim reaper I strove to become. Maybe I wasn't a badass yet, but at least I wasn't a bumbling idiot anymore. Plus, I now possessed the mega cool ability to reap supernatural creatures because I was the granddaughter of Death. Sure, it was something like eleven-million times removed, but it still counted, therefore I got the choicest reaper swag. Thanks, Hal. He'd kill me if I ever called him grandpa.

I headed into the building and took the elevator directly to the seventh-floor Command Center. When the metal doors slid open, chaos bombarded me. The noise level ratcheted up, people yelling out orders. They called it the *Halloween Crazy* because it was Grim Reaper Services busiest night of the year. Every ghost, ghoul, and idiot came out of the woodwork on Halloween.

For me, the holiday was pure hell. My clients were people who died in idiotic ways. Nate referred to my assignments as miscellaneous reaps. I called most of them morons, and Halloween only helped magnify my opinion. Many people went out of their way to be reaped by yours truly, performing epic feats of stupidity no sane person would attempt. Like snowmobiling across the thin ice with pumpkins on their heads. Dumb and dead. It was as if Fate had created Halloween especially for me. Thanks, Fate.

Not all of them were idiots. For instance, I once reaped a woman who was killed by a runaway-shopping cart. When it hit her, the cart pushed her into oncoming traffic. Completely not her fault, but it still fell to me to send her on. Sometimes reaping sucked.

I joined my rock solid and fiercely gorgeous boss, Constantine, on the riser in the center of the room. Radars lined the platform, and currently, dozens of green blips bopped around the screens. Each blip represented a person, and for whatever reason, they were slated to die. Reapers rarely got a close-up view of the screens. It was GRS's policy to keep us in the dark until our client's scheduled time of death arrived. That way we wouldn't be able to prevent it. Knowing myself all too well, that was a prudent procedure to have in place.

"Hey there." I smiled and shoved my hands in the back pockets of my jeans. I'll be honest, I couldn't trust myself around him. Whenever I got near Constantine, the urge to lean into him and let my hands wander over his body nearly swallowed me. The only thing that kept me from acting on the impulse was fear. He possessed a very otherworldly vibe, and I wasn't sure he was actually human. I'd learned firsthand that a variety of paranormal creatures existed. I didn't know where he fit into the picture—and I wasn't sure I wanted to find out. "What's the special assignment?" Instead of looking at him, I kept my eyes fixed on the green dots. "I don't have to reap a troll or something like that, do I?"

"Not tonight, Carron." Unable to stop my eyes from wandering to his face, my gaze slid to him. He had grayish-silver eyes that I could fall into, and creamy brown skin that reminded me of a perfect cup of coffee. "Let's go into my office. Nate will meet us there in a minute."

A tremor skittered down my spine when he wrapped his fingers around my upper arm. My gaze traveled from his face to his hand. His grip was gentle but firm, and when he maneuvered me toward his office, our bodies touched. Heat raced along my hip and thigh. Yowza, it had been way too long since I'd received any serious male attention, and I suspected I projected that onto Constantine.

At six feet something, he dwarfed me, making me feel feminine. That in itself was quite an achievement and probably made him all the more attractive. I knew it was pathetic, but it was all I had.

He released me as we neared his office door and then led the way inside. With a businesslike wave toward the chairs, he indicated I should sit—so I did because that's what a smart person did when Constantine told them to do something—followed orders.

The door closing sounded behind me, and a few seconds later, my partner Nate dropped into the black leather chair next to me. "Hey, Carron."

"Hey, Cramer." My relationship with Nate had grown into something comfortable, like an old pair of shoes. Though, I secretly wished it was a lot sexier than that—it wasn't. He'd kissed me once, but that was because I'd exorcised a pretty nasty demon from him. So, more a kiss of gratitude than lust. Though we kept things platonic, there was no denying he was nice to look at. I lifted my eyebrows in question. "Do you know what this special assignment is?"

"No." He shook his head. "But with our luck, it will be unpleasant."

"No doubt."

"It won't be so bad." Constantine shoved a file toward us. "All you have to do is capture the ghost of Samuel Parker."

"Who's Samuel Parker?" Nate asked.

Constantine motioned toward the file. I opened it to reveal an old colored eight-by-ten photo of a handsome thirty-something man. Alluring dark features stared back at me. Black hair, brown eyes, high cheekbones, straight nose. If I hadn't already known who Samuel Parker was, I might have been excited about wrangling this particular spirit.

"Samuel Parker used to own the City Center Theater," I said, glancing at Constantine. "Built it, as a matter of fact, right?"

"Yeah." He leaned back in his chair and folded his hands over his flat stomach. "What else do you know about him?"

"He was charming, wealthy, and one of the elite in Anchorage society during the fifties."

Nate shrugged. "Doesn't sound too bad. So, what's the catch?"

"The catch is," I continued, "that Samuel Parker was thought to be a serial killer. Three women, I think, right?"

"Four," Constantine corrected. "You'll find all the history and police reports in that file, so brush up on it before you head to the theater."

"Wait." Dread poured over me. "We have to go into the theater?"

"Yes." He arched a black brow. "Is there a problem?"

"Uh, yeah." Scooting as far from the file as I could, I leaned back in my chair. "It's only the creepiest, most haunted place in town."

"You're a grim reaper, Carron."

"Why do you always say that like it means anything? Just because I'm a reaper doesn't mean I can't get hurt, or in this case, die. Remember—serial killer?"

"You'll be fine." He waved away my argument. "Nate will keep you safe."

My lips pinched into a constricted smile and I glanced at my partner. There was no doubt he was a skilled reaper, but over the months, I'd proven I was every bit as good—maybe even better because of my ability to reap the paranormal. There were things I could do that no other reaper could. He stared at me as if waiting for my objection. I forced my smile to widen but kept silent. No need to stir up trouble, after all, I actually did want him to protect me if I needed it.

At one time, the City Center Theater had been the social hotspot for plays and performances. Though many people had moved to Alaska for adventure, or because they were running from something, i.e. the law, they'd insisted on maintaining the social standards they had in the lower forty-eight. But after a string of murders, a few of which took place right in the theater, the City Center Theater had closed and never reopened.

"The current owner, Lizzy Git, will meet you at the back entrance at five o'clock. That will give you time to look around and set up." Constantine tapped the file. "Familiarize yourself with this stuff. It might come in handy."

I shuffled through the pictures. The next four after Parker's photo were young women. It looked as if all the pictures had been taken sometime in the fifties. The last photo was of an older woman, maybe pushing forty, dressed in bellbottom pants, a peasant blouse, and a brown leather headband. She reminded me of Janice Joplin and looked like she was straight out of the sixties. I angled the photo in order to read the name written on the bottom.

"Evelyn Git?" My gaze cut to Constantine. "Any relationship to the current owner?"

"Aunt," He replied. "She used to be quite the socialite and party thrower. It was never a problem until her 1963 Halloween bash." Leaning against the chair again, he resumed his folded hand pose. "It's a cold case, but her niece suspects she met her demise at the hands of Samuel

Parker."

During my time as a grim reaper, more than my fair share of ghosts had beaten me around. It didn't surprise me to hear that Parker had continued his killing spree beyond the grave. Surprised? No. Scared? Yes. A little sick to my stomach at the thought of spending the night in the theater? Definitely.

"We got this." Nate closed the folder and stood, tucking the file under his arm. "We'll keep you posted on our progress."

"Yeah." I stood and gave Constantine a smile I didn't feel. He was never quite as good looking when he sent me into one of these dangerous and possibly fatal situations. "Unless…you know…we're dead."

He returned a grin. "Report back anyway—even if you're dead."

"So heartless."

I trailed Nate out of the office and stomped across the Command Center to the elevator. This really wasn't fair. I'd followed procedure and blocked vacation time off on the calendar. My friend, Vella, and I had made plans. We were going to dress up in fuzzy pajamas, and then to ensure a stellar candy haul, we'd take the boys trick-or-treating through the rich neighborhoods. Then, while the boys gorged themselves on sweets and watched Halloween cartoons, we were going to drink wine, hand out candy and heckle the teenagers who didn't bother dressing up.

My night had been planned. Staking out a haunted theater and the very real threat of death was not what I'd banked on for Halloween.

CHAPTER TWO

Gravel crunched under my tires as I turned off the alley and into the parking lot behind the theater. Other than being painted a salmon-color, the back of the building had no definable character. Most of the glitz and glam had been saved for the front facade, but even that showed major signs of decline.

Thin rectangular windows ran in four rows along the flat concrete wall, all of them dark, and all of them extra creepy. My gaze darted away from the upper row in case there were any shadowy specters watching my arrival. It's one thing to take a spirit by surprise and reap it. It's another to see them watching and waiting for you.

A shiver raced along my spine, and I reached across the seat to grip the black cylinder nestled against my bag. Some people had their blankets for comfort. I had my scythe. It had been a gift from my porter Hal, who was also my great, great, great whatever grandfather. His real name was Thanatos, the original Death, and he'd once enjoyed a stint as the first ferryman on the River Styx. Now Charon, son of Nyx and Erebus, as well as being Hal's brother, did the ferrying. Long story—lots of family drama.

My fingers caressed the intricate carvings around

the upper edge of the cylinder. Knowing this bad boy could reap the darkest demon from Hell gave me comfort and bolstered my determination to take down Samuel Parker. Sure, he was a serial killer, but I'd dealt with worse—a lot worse. No doubt there would be other ghosts lurking about the theater. I wasn't foolish enough to think this would be a one-and-done assignment.

Thankfully, Nate had already arrived. He waited in his vehicle, so I pulled in beside him, and then got out. A gravelly squawk broadcasted above me, drawing my attention back to the building's roof. Perched on the ledge sat a fat black raven.

Anchorage has some of the biggest ravens known to man, and my familiar, Fletcher, led the pack in heftiness. I was partly to blame for him being the size of a Welsh Corgi. After connecting as reaper and familiar, I felt compelled to leave him a daily treat. To be honest, I suspected Fletcher was using some kind of raven mind control on me because every day around the same time, the idea to give him a treat popped into my head. If I didn't instantly set out the kibble, the image of him would continue to appear in my mind until I did. So really, it would be his fault if one day he couldn't heft his body off his perch. I could just see him catching a ride with me to my reaps. Yeah, nothing weird about a raven in a booster seat, being driven around by a hockey mom. I made a mental note to toss out his bird treats.

Whether he'd come in hopes of getting a snack or to help me, I was glad he was here. I fingered the raven pendant at my neck and the sensation of wings brushing against me fluttered along my entire body. I smiled and closed my driver door.

Though the extent of our communication wasn't much more than his squawks, letting me know he'd arrived or something was amiss, there did always seem to be a mental flow between us. I called it the *knowing*. I always knew what he was trying to tell me, no matter how vague. Fletcher had given me the pendant before I'd ever agreed to be a reaper. Guess he'd known more than I had. The necklace gave me an extra supernatural zap when I needed it, and boy, had I needed it.

I walked around to Nate's side and he rolled down his window. Not one for small talk or pleasantries, he got straight to business. "Ms. Git isn't here yet."

"No hurry as far as I'm concerned," I said, rubbing my arms against the October bite. It hadn't snowed yet, but the crisp nip in the air smelled as if it could any day. I tapped on my step-tracker, lighting up the time. "We still have five minutes."

"Climb in." He cocked his head toward the passenger side of his SUV and smiled. "No need to freeze while we wait."

Nate had dimples, and when he smiled, they deepened, making him hella attractive. I guess I should consider myself lucky to be working with him. I won't lie, he was bikini-waxing worthy, but we kept our relationship strictly professional—at least I thought that's what we were doing. There had been times when he'd looked at me a certain way, or said something that could have easily been misconstrued as interest, but it never went any farther.

He'd been my dead husband's partner before he'd become mine, and I'm sure that had something to do with it. What's that saying, bros before hos? Except his bro was dead, so I didn't see how it applied. Still, we were reapers, and we never knew when somebody from the past who had passed, might come knocking on our door.

I climbed into the Suburban and sighed when the blasting heat hit me and melted away my shivers. "Did you get a chance to look at the file?" I asked.

"Briefly scanned it." He handed me the folder. "It seems Samuel only makes an appearance once a year."

"Let me guess, on Halloween?" I flipped open the file.

"Exactly. That's why we were assigned to it tonight and not earlier this year." He twisted in the seat and leaned against the door, resting his arm across the steering wheel. "And Carron—" No humor lurked in his expression. "The guy has a real thing for blondes." He paused. "Just sayin'."

"Oh, great." My eyes darted to him and I pointed at my head. "Can't get much blonder than this."

"You might want to stick close to me tonight. I don't want him getting the drop on you."

I ignored the happy flutter his comment incited. "Wow, that almost sounded like concern."

Though I hated to admit it, Nate was the only person in my life who looked out for my physical wellbeing, and that did things to my insides—things I didn't want to analyze too deeply.

"Of course I'm concerned." A smirk curled the corner of his lip, accentuating his dimple. "Concerned I'm going to have to train a new partner."

"Well, if I do die…" I pulled my gaze from his face and returned it to the file. "I'm coming back to haunt you. I'm going to sit right here and chatter away non-stop."

"So…" He nodded. "Pretty much like usual."

A snort of laughter erupted from me, but that was all the response I gave his insult. I flipped over the first photo and read the back. "Irene White. It says she was his stepsister, and his first murder victim in 1955." Turning the picture over again, I stared at the woman grinning back at me. "She's beautiful—was beautiful." I shook my head. "What kind of monster murders his own sister?"

"The serial killer kind." Nate leaned across the seat and angled his head to see the photo. Mint mingled with the smell of his soap and tickled my nose, tempting me to lean into him. Instead, I shifted the picture closer so he could see better, and forced my body to stay where it was. "Maybe she knew what he was," he continued as if the warm cab and close quarters totally weren't creating sexual tension between us. "And he silenced her before she could tell."

"Maybe." My answer came out a bit breathy, so I cleared my throat and shuffled to the next photo. "Pammy Caldwell, murdered May 1956 inside the City Center Theater." My shoulders sagged. "Great, no doubt she'll be floating around in there tonight."

"Pammy was an actress, an understudy for the main star, and only nineteen when she was murdered, so I wouldn't doubt it." Nate pulled the last photo from the bottom of the stack. "And this is Carolyn Turner, Samuel Parker's longtime girlfriend. Supposedly, he murdered her in 1957 and then killed himself." He paused and looked at me. "Right here in the theater."

"Awesome." Tonight just kept getting better and better. I scrutinized Carolyn Turner. She looked like a Marilyn Monroe wannabe. Too bad her rising star had been snuffed out so early. "So, Parker killed her and then killed himself?"

"That's what the police report said."

I shook my head. "That doesn't make sense. If he was a serial killer, wouldn't he want to keep killing?"

"Evidently not. Maybe it was one of those weird suicide pacts." He settled back in the seat. "There isn't a lot of information surrounding their deaths, but tons about their lives. Carolyn was the lead actress at the theater, and Samuel was the wealthy owner."

"A match made in Heaven," I said.

"Or Hell." Nate glanced in the rearview mirror. "Lizzy Git is here."

My stomach lurched, sending a wave of dread through me. I inhaled and forced myself to open the car door and exit the warmth—and safety—of the Suburban.

Lizzy Git looked a lot like her dead aunt's photo. She wore no makeup and her blond hair frizzed in all directions, giving her an earthy appearance—just the kind of woman I imagined Nate going for. "Mr. Cramer?" She smiled brightly, her big brown eyes sparkling with outward appreciation. She extended her right hand. "I'm Lizzy Git."

"Nice to meet you." Nate shook her hand and then turned toward me. "This is my partner, Lisa Carron."

"Hello." Her smile dimmed slightly, but she offered me her hand.

"Hi." I shook it twice and let go, not saying anything more. Neither Constantine nor Nate had explained how much Ms. Git knew about us, so I let lover boy take the lead. Otherwise, I'd no doubt stick my foot in my mouth.

"I sure hope you guys can do something about the haunting." Her mouth and brows pinch simultaneously. "We'd planned on renovating and reopening the theater a few years ago, but weird accidents kept happening and people got hurt." Her face relaxed. "My family and I thought it was better to cut our losses before any real damage was done. Besides taxes and the utilities, the building doesn't cost us. Not as much as a lawsuit would."

"That was probably smart," Nate said. "But hopefully, we'll be able to clear out any unpleasant spirits tonight."

"Constantine was kind of vague when he said he knew people who could help." Her eyes tracked to me and then back to him. "So, are you guys like…Ghostbusters or something?"

"Something like that." Turning on the charm, Nate hit her with one of his smiles. "We're more like cleaners."

A giggle tittered from her. "I'm sure you're really good at your job."

I repressed the urge to roll my eyes and make a gagging sound. Instead, I patiently waited for the two of them to stop ogling each other, which was a fraction more preferable than heading into the theater of death.

"City Center Theater has been in my family since my aunt bought it in 1962. After she was murdered at a Halloween party she hosted, it was passed to my uncle—then to his son—another cousin—" She paused and shrugged. "—Well, the truth is, I inherited it because nobody else wanted it. But I truly believe it could be spectacular again if…well, you know… it gets cleaned up."

"We'll do our best to make that happen for you," Nate said.

She continued to smile at him and didn't appear to have any intention of unlocking the door. I wasn't jealous of her obvious infatuation with Nate—I seriously wasn't—but my damn toes were getting cold.

"All right then." I rounded my eyes and clapped my

hands once. "Let's go check out this glorious theater, shall we?"

"Of course." She started a bit and then lurched forward as if she'd been poked with an electric prod. "I'll unlock the door and leave you to it. No sense in me getting in your way."

"Yeah, that would probably be best," I agreed a little louder than I intended. Nate frowned at me. I returned his glower and mouthed, "What?"

Of course, it was a rhetorical question, but his stare lasted about three seconds longer than was necessary, driving home the point that he thought I was being rude. Hey, she was the one who said she wasn't coming in. I just agreed with her.

I grabbed my bag and scythe cylinder out of my car and jogged to catch up with them. I'd made sure to stock my essentials for reaping; scythe, phone, hat and gloves in case it was cold inside, a bottle of water, and the two-pound bag of Halloween candy I'd bought for trick-or-treaters. What? I couldn't leave the candy sitting on the counter. It looked so lonely and dejected.

After pawing through the mass of keys on the large ring, Lizzy finally found the right one and unlocked the back door. The hinges squeaked in protest when she pulled it open, and the musty smell that reminded me of my grandmother's attic hit us.

She stepped back. "There you go. Lights to most of the backstage are right inside the door. Throw the big lever and it will turn on enough lights for you to maneuver through the theater. Each area and room has its own panel just inside the door if you need more lights."

I peered into the darkness. It was really, really, really dark in there. Hopefully, she'd tucked away extra cash for utilities this month, because I had every intention of lighting up the inside of City Center Theater like it was midnight in Times Square.

"We've got it from here," Nate said. From inside his backpack, he pulled out the biggest flashlight I'd ever seen. The flat front was the size of a small dinner plate, and when he flicked it on, it nearly blinded me. "Constantine will give you a call tomorrow and let you know how things go."

"Okay." Her voice trembled. "You're sure you'll be all right?"

"We'll be fine." He laid a hand on her shoulder and my smile pulled a tad bit tighter. "We do this kind of work all the time."

I was glad he was so confident; because even the million-candle-watt monster flashlight hadn't chased away the feeling of impending doom gnawing at me.

"All right then." Her eyes cut to me. From the uncertainty playing across her face, the woman clearly had no confidence in my abilities. "But call me if you need anything." She descended one step. "Even if it's one o'clock in the morning."

"Thank you, Ms. Git, but I'm sure we'll be fine." Wow, I actually sounded like I meant that.

She nodded, turned, and jogged down the concrete steps. Before pulling out of the parking lot, she gave us a stilted wave. I knew how she felt. Just because I was a grim reaper didn't mean I was brave. It simply meant I was stupid. I pivoted and followed Nate into the theater of death—and possibly my own demise.

CHAPTER THREE

Backstage of the theater was about forty times scarier than when I was standing outside looking in. Every rope, mop, and prop looked like a hovering specter, waiting to pounce.

"Tell me again why I agreed to work for GRS," I said, pulling the door closed behind me.

"Great benefits." Nate stopped and swung the flashlight left to right. "And you needed a job."

"Oh yeah, money." As casually as possible, I inched closer to him. He'd told me to stick by him tonight, and I planned on taking that to heart. "Where's the light panel?"

"There." The blaze from the flashlight landed on a large metal box hanging against the far wall. He moved toward it. Clutching my bag to me, I shuffled after him. Another loud squeak echoed through the backstage when he pulled the breaker box open. What was it with creepy places and squeaky hinges? It was like you couldn't have one without the other. "Let's hope this does the trick."

He wrestled a long lever at the side of the box upward. Sweet glory, the backstage lights flared to life, and everything that had once been uber scary in the dark took its true nonthreatening form.

"Nice job." I held up my hand for a high-five.

Nate's eyes cut from my hand to my face. "Come on, don't leave a partner hanging."

He stared at me as if I was acting sophomoric. Didn't he know the importance of bonding during life-or-death situations? This definitely qualified. He walked past me, leaving me unhigh-fived. I spun and glared at his back. Not demonstrating proper partner etiquette was like slapping me across each cheek with a glove. Challenge accepted! By the end of the evening, Nate Cramer would show me appropriate partner camaraderie, or I might have to reap him.

Backstage was big, but the auditorium was ten times that size. Pink upholstered seats spread up the slanted floor and along two upper balcony rows. The dim interior faded to dark shadowed corners at the edges of the palatial room. We stood at the center of the stage, neither of us speaking, taking in the expanse of the theater.

After a minute, I said, "I've never been interested in acting, but I get it."

"Get what?" Nate walked to the edge and looked into the orchestra pit.

"The thrill of being up here in front of a packed house." I joined him, also staring into the dark pit. "Performing. Hearing the cheers after you've put your heart and soul into your performance."

"Sadly, Parker took that a little too literally." He straightened. "Let's check out the lobby."

"All right." Slinging my bag across my body, I tromped behind him. As we made our way up the aisle, I dug inside and tore open the bag of Halloween candy. Sugar always made me feel better. "Want some?" I held out a handful of mini candy bars to him. "I've got a whole bag."

He didn't even glance down, just kept walking. "No thanks."

"Seriously?" I shoved my hand toward him again, certain he hadn't heard me correctly. I mean, this was Halloween candy. "It's Halloween candy. Nobody turns down Halloween candy."

"I do."

"Suit yourself, freak." The crinkling wrappers sounded exceptionally loud in the silent theater. I caught the disgruntled look and barely contained sneer Nate shot at me but preferred to ignore him. Nobody could stop me from enjoying my candy. Not Nate. Not ghosts. Not even a serial killer. Yeah, I meant business when it came to Halloween. "More for me."

He quickened his pace, and I had to jog to keep up with him, but still managed to unwrap three tiny candy bars before we made it to the foyer.

Though I'd seen old photographs of the City Center Theater at the museum, I hadn't expected it to be so grand. My eyes tracked upward to the opulent chandelier hanging sixty feet above us. He let out a long whistle. "That's a lot of crystal."

"And mirrors." Eight-foot-tall mirrors framed in gilded gold hung between each arch leading into the theater. Below the mirrors, art deco torch-lights cast a yellow glow onto the frames, making them glisten. "And gold." I walked to the spiral staircase and bent to eye the gold ornate railing. "Do you think it's real?"

"If it was real, somebody would have stolen it by now."

"True." I straightened. "Too bad."

"Why? You planning on a little larceny, Carron."

"It might clash with my 1970s split-level décor." Gliding back to where he stood, I let my gaze travel around the expanse of the room. "Just trying to get a feel for Samuel Parker."

"It doesn't appear as if money was a problem."

"I'd say." I turned to him. "So, what now?"

"Let's find a place to store our stuff. Somewhere centrally located in case we get separated."

"Well, let's not get separated." I swallowed down the lump of fear that rose in my throat. "Remember that whole loves-to-kill-blondes thing?"

"I remember." His gaze leveled on me, and he gently gripped my shoulder. "Don't worry, Carron, I'll protect you." There was that little flutter again, the one that made me too aware of his blue eyes and broad chest. "If you don't do something stupid, like trying to reap Samuel alone."

Aaaaand, then the mood was broken. I shook off his hands. "Not a problem. Being alone with Samuel Parker ranks right up there with oral surgery." Crossing my arms over my chest, I stuck out my hip and glared at him. "Besides, I don't do stupid stuff."

"Las Vegas? Ferrying the dead without telling me. Fighting demons." He tapped my head with his index finger. "Any of this ringing a bell?"

"Uhhh, excuse me, saving mankind, being a team player. If that's what you're talking about, then I guess I'm guilty."

Okay, so one time I hadn't clued Nate into the bigger picture, and now he was going to hold it against me forever. It wasn't my fault I'd been the only one who could have pulled off the job. Besides, the bigwigs at GRS told me not to tell anybody. And when I say bigwigs, I'm talking about beings from both upstairs and downstairs. Who knew Heaven and Hell worked together to maintain balance? Anyway, this was not Vegas, and I had no intention of cozying up with Samuel Parker.

"Let's look for a room, somewhere not so out in the open."

"Good call." I straightened. "Maybe a dressing room."

"Right." Nate headed toward the theater again.

Trailing after him, I glanced at one of the gilded mirrors hanging beside the arched doorway and stopped. A woman stood in the reflected opening, watching us. She was young and blond, probably not much older than twenty. Our eyes met, and I recognized her. Pammy Caldwell. That had to be an all-time record. In the haunted place for five minutes and I'd already had my first ghost sighting.

After a few seconds, she faded away. It didn't matter how long I'd been a grim reaper, seeing spirits still gave me a jolt of surprise, and that would probably never change. I blew out a breath and rubbed my arms, trying to extinguish the shiver streaming through my body.

Corridors branched off in a labyrinth of halls and rooms. Thankfully, Nate opted to set up camp in one of the first rooms on the left.

"Good call." I scanned the area, moving deeper into it. "This looks like the cast break room." No sense in delving deeper into the bowels of the sinister theater just yet. There would be plenty of that on our nightly schedule. I dropped my bag onto the hunter green velvet couch, triggering a puff of dust from the cushion. The cloud shot into my face and made my nose tingle. I waved away the ancient swirl of filth and then sneezed. I'm allergic to dust—well, actually, I'm allergic to cleaning—or maybe I'm just opposed to cleaning—still, I don't like dust. "I think I just inhaled five decades of dust motes."

"That's nasty." Expending the bulk of his sympathy on that one statement, Nate set his backpack on a long wooden table and then walked to the row of cabinets at the end of the room. "It's like this place has been frozen in time." He opened the first door and pulled out a familiar dark blue tin with yellow writing. "Spam. I bet it's still good."

"It was never good." I flared my nostrils and pointed a warning finger at him. "Don't even think about opening that or I'll yak up right here."

"This might save our lives if we get trapped." He turned back to the cabinet. "I wonder if there's any Pilot

Bread."

Pilot Bread was an Alaskan staple, large Saltine-looking crackers with a fraction of the taste and a hundred times the toughness. Dressed up with a thick slab of Spam, a person could survive for weeks on a container of each, as long as they had enough water to choke the delicacies down.

"I'll pass, thanks." Spinning in a slow circle, I surveyed the room. He was right about the place being frozen in time. Old Playbill theater posters hung on the wall. Guys and Dolls, South Pacific, and my favorite, Seven Brides for Seven Brothers. Faded turquoise walls still gave the room a festive feel which was good, because beyond the break room door was a whole lot of spookiness. "So, I think we should check out the upper balconies first."

He turned to me, his eyes laser focused. "Why? Did you see something?"

"I think Pammy Caldwell hangs out up there. Maybe she's got info about Samuel."

"If we can get her to talk."

I nodded. "That's always the first hurdle, isn't it?" Finding spirits never seemed to be a problem. "She's young and was an actress. I doubt we'll have trouble getting her to talk once she trusts us."

"Well, it's a place to start."

I pulled my scythe cylinder out of my bag and hooked it to the belt loop on my jeans. More than likely I wouldn't need the extra reaping power, but I didn't want to take any chances.

Nate led the way out of the break room and through the theater. It still appeared empty, but the sensation of being watched followed me. I scanned the balcony, but there wasn't enough light to make anything or anyone out.

Thick rose-colored carpet covered the wide spiraling staircase and cushioned our footsteps. We climbed to the second level where I'd seen Pammy and entered the theater through the first door labeled Section *A-B*.

The level curved in a semi-circle around the back and sides of the theater, with doors position at every fifth row. Below, the stage spread across the front of the house floor, and anybody sitting in these prime seats would have gotten the whole view of the performance. We walked along the upper aisle, both of us searching the balcony for any hint of spirit activity.

Near the center, the feeling of being watched hit me again. This time stronger and closer. I pivoted, my breath catching in my throat. Pammy Caldwell floated several yards away, staring at me with fearful curiosity, and looking as if she'd just stepped off a 1950's movie set. The white blouse she wore sported a Peter Pan collar, and her pink cardigan matched the band firmly lodged in her teased up, flipped out blond hair.

"Pammy?" I pitched my voice higher than normal and smiled. It was the same voice I'd used on my mom's dog when she escaped the house and I tried to get her back in. Slowly, I edged toward her. "My name is Lisa."

She drifted backward a couple of feet. Not wanting to freak her out, I stopped. A quiet brush of carpet sounded behind me and then Nate's breath tickled my neck. "Easy," he whispered.

Never taking my eyes from Pammy, I nodded once. "Would you mind talking to us?"

Her eyes narrowed. "About what?"

Discussing her death probably wasn't the best way to start a conversation. Some ghosts don't even realize they're dead. It's one of those subjects I try to ease into. "The theater and acting."

"I'm an actress." She pressed her hands to her chest, her face lighting up. Her translucent body levitated a couple of inches higher, solidifying slightly. "I was the lead in all my high school plays."

"I bet you were wonderful," I said.

"The paper did an article, saying I had a bright future in acting. That's how Mr. Parker found out about me."

Bingo, nice segue. "So, you auditioned for him?"

"Yes, ma'am. I was Miss Turner's understudy." Her smile faded. "Well...until I died."

"Pammy." I took a couple of slow steps toward her. "Do you know how that happened?"

"I don't want to talk about it." Her expression darkened, her brows pinching together and her mouth drawing into a straight line.

I knew I was pushing, but I tried my best mom psychobabble. "It might help you feel better."

Her hands cupped her neck, and she shook her head. "No. I don't like to think about that."

"Wait." Short of grabbing her, which was one of my reaper skills, I couldn't stop her from leaving. Her image grew nearly transparent. "I want to help you, Pammy." She continued to shake her head and then completely disappeared. I stomped my foot and propped my fists on my hips. "Well, crap."

"Maybe she'll come back." Nate's hand settled on my shoulder, sending a wave of warmth through me. "She seemed eager to talk about herself."

"She did, didn't she?" I sighed and turned to face him. Though his hand fell away, we still stood about a foot apart—twelve tiny inches. Our eyes locked, and my breath caught in my throat. He was too good looking for his own good—for my own good. If his respect for me as a partner didn't matter so much, I might have planted one on him. Damn my work ethics. "Now what?"

"Keep searching." He continued to stare at me but didn't make a move to *keep searching*. For a second, I thought we were going to have that moment I'd fantasized about a thousand times. Then he cleared his throat and took a step back. "For other spirits."

"Yeah, we should totally do that." I waited, trying to use the power of my mind to compel him to make a move, but he didn't. One day I'd master that skill.

"Right." He pivoted and strode away, leaving me staring at his back.

A sigh of longing slipped from me. Was I attracted to Nate? Definitely. Was he attracted to me? I had no idea, but even if there was a spark between us, he'd mentally set me off limits because of my dead husband—his partner.

Giving myself a mental shake, I refocused on our mission. We had a serial killer to catch, and as much as I didn't want to admit it, that was more important than my love life.

CHAPTER FOUR

We wandered in and out of rooms, down halls, and into the darkest depths of the theater with no luck. Not a single ghost showed. Back in the break room, I dropped onto the couch, forgetting about the decades of dust, and got blasted again. Waving away the cloud, I said, "At this rate, it's going to be a boring night."

"Yeah, Pammy is the only spirit we know for sure that is here." Perching on the edge of the table, he crossed his arms over his chest and his feet at the ankles. "We need to draw her out."

"How?"

"I don't know." He hesitated. "What do twentyish women like?"

"Clothes, makeup, selfies, boys, talking about themselves." An idea popped into my head. "What if we go snoop around the wardrobe room?"

"What's that going to do?"

"Maybe nothing, but it's someplace to start." What girl didn't love to play dress-up? That might just draw Pammy out.

We exited and continued down the hall to where the costumes for the plays were kept. Like the break room, the wardrobe room looked as if it had been frozen in time. Boas, capes and every piece of clothing known to mankind hung on racks or were draped over sewing mannequins.

A tiny squeak eeped from me when I entered the room. Normally, I'm not one for shopping, and I'm certainly not girlie, but the array of fabrics and colors would have tried any woman's resolve.

"Man, look at all this stuff." Nate yanked a hanger off the rack and held up a foot-long swath of fur. "Loincloth?"

"Hmm." I scratched my chin. "I can't be sure. Try it on."

He snorted. "You wish."

"You have no idea," I mumbled, turning away from him.

"So, what now?"

"How about a fashion show?"

He shook his head. "I already told you I'm not putting on that fur flap."

"Such a shame." A rack of gowns hung against the far wall. I ran my hand along the collection of chiffon and taffeta, finally deciding on a royal blue creation that would have quickened the heartbeat of any young actress. "Perfect."

"Are you planning on putting that on?" Nate started toward me, but I held up my hand.

"Stay." I hitched my thumb toward the changing screen. "I'll be right back."

"And you're doing this why?"

"Call it a hunch." I ducked behind the screen and stripped. The thing I loved about vintage clothes were their real woman curves. I'd toned up and lost some weight after joining GRS, but I would always be curvy. The dress slipped over my head and down my hips, instantly transforming me into a starlet. After stepping from behind the screen, I twirled. "What do you think?"

"Wow." A couple of sounds that weren't quite words sputtered from him. "You look fantastic. Right off the stage."

"Thank you." His compliment warmed me all the way down to my toes. Centering myself in front of a three-way mirror, I turned right and left. "I wonder what play this was for."

"Kiss me, Kate," said a gravelly female voice directly behind me.

Nearly jumping out of my skin, I pivoted toward the door. At first, I didn't see anybody, but slowly the image of a woman materialized. Short and round, she appeared to be pushing sixty. A measuring tape hung around her neck, and crystal-tipped cat-eyed glasses perched on the end of her nose. She peered at us over the top, drawing on a long pink cigarette holder.

The need to apologize hit me. "Sorry, I couldn't resist trying it on."

"I made it for Miss Turner." Still pinching the cigarette, she flicked her hand dismissively in the air. "Never wore it though. She said the cut was wrong. Like she knew anything about fashion." She took a long draw on her cigarette again and blew out the spectral smoke. "If it wasn't showing off her assets—" The ghost gestured toward her chest. "—Then she didn't want anything to do with it."

"Well, I think it's beautiful," I said, as if talking to a ghost happened every day, which it usually did. "My name is Lisa, and this is Nate." Though she didn't seem skittish like Pammy's ghost had, playing it cool might keep her talking. "You are?"

"Arlene Daily, head costumer and master seamstress." She blew out more smoke, which was weird because she hadn't taken another drag, and then floated toward us. "At least I used to be."

So far, each spirit seemed aware of their situation,

which made our job a lot easier. No big *"ta-da, you're dead"* reveal. "It must have been quite an experience to work here in its heyday."

"At first, sure." She stopped next to a dress mannequin and adjusted a white feather boa around the neck. "Everybody got along. The actors acted because they loved their craft."

"It sounds like that didn't last." Nate settled against the table again, but his eyes never left Arlene. From the set of his shoulders and straightness of his spine, I knew he was in the hyper-vigilant mode. Ever since his demon possession, he never let his guard down in the presence of a spirit. Personally, the only thing threatening about Arlene seemed to be her sharp tongue. "What happened?"

"Not what, who." Tipping her head down, she peered at him over her glasses. "Carolyn Turner. Talk about a drama queen." She sashayed toward us, flipping her hands against imaginary long hair. Her voice rose several octaves. "Arlene, darling, I can't possibly wear this shade of blue. I can't possibly be seen in this monstrosity. I can't possibly meet my fans wearing this." Lowering her hands, her face melted into a deadpan stare. "You know what else she couldn't possibly do? Act, that's what."

"She sounds horrible," I said.

"She was the worst," Arlene agreed. "Just because she was from California, she thought she was all that. Poor Mr. Parker." Her lips pursed as if she'd sucked on a lemon. "The way she wrapped him around her diamond encrusted finger made me want to beat him about the head and pound some sense into the man."

Poor Mr. Parker? Okay, not quite the way I would have described him, but at least Arlene had brought up the very subject I'd been hedging toward. "Speaking of dying, Arlene. You weren't murdered by chance..." I gave her a tight smile. "Were you?"

"Heart attack." Pointing to a spot on the floor, she sighed. "One minute I was munching on my apple pastry, the next, boom, flat out on the floor."

"I'm so sorry," I said, meaning it.

Her shoulders lifted and then dropped. "Meh, there are worse ways to die. Besides the sharp pain in my chest, I didn't feel a thing."

"Can I ask why you've hung around?" Nate chimed in, resuming his crossed ankle pose, probably realizing Arlene wasn't dangerous. "Why not move on?"

"At first I hung around to make sure somebody found me. Then I stayed to make sure everything went smoothly for the play." She took a long draw on her cigarette. Though the tip glowed red, the ash didn't seem to get longer. Maybe it was an afterlife perk. Blowing out, the white cloud circled her head. "Before I knew it, a decade had passed," she continued, "There are so many spirits in this place, nobody had noticed the theater had actually closed down."

"What about Samuel Parker?" I inched toward Arlene. Maybe she could give us a solid lead on how to find him. "Is he around here?

"Only on Halloween." Her mouth turned down in a frown, and she shook her head. "But, he's usually busy."

"Busy with what?" Nate moved to stand next to me.

"Unpleasant things happen on Halloween." A visible shudder rippled through the ghost, and she rubbed her arms as if cold. "Some of us who worked here make ourselves scarce."

"What about tonight?" Secretly, I prayed she hadn't seen him. If he knew we were here, then he'd probably been watching us—watching me. "Have you seen him?"

"You're the only ones I've seen so far tonight." Shoving her free hand into the pocket of her blue smock, she retreated a couple of feet. "I wanted to warn you before things got weird. You should probably leave."

"We're hoping things get weird," Nate said. "That's

why we're here."

"I can see you're nervous about tonight, Arlene." I held out a hand, keeping my palm turned upward. In one of GRS's reaper trainings, we'd been coached on how to deal with spirits. Open hands were supposed to instill trust. "My partner and I can help you pass to the other side if you'd like."

"What are you?" Her gaze narrowed. "Angels or something?"

"Actually." I kept my hand extended and widened my smile. "We're grim reapers."

Her eyes cut from me to Nate and back again. "I expected Death to be more…horrifying."

"Yeah, well," Nate said, "think of us as kinder, gentler grim reapers."

"We're not going to have a group hug, are we?" she asked.

"Not if I can help it," Nate said.

"Don't go," came a familiar voice behind me. We all turned to see Pammy floating near the far corner. She looked like a scared anime character, her blue eyes rounded to twice their normal size. "Don't leave me here by myself, Arlene."

I faced her. "We can help you cross too, Pammy."

"No." Wringing her hands together, she shook her head. "I can't go. Not yet."

"Pammy, sweetie." Arlene's tone took on a motherly concern. "You don't have to stay here."

"Yes, I do." She sniffed and lifted her chin. "I need to know."

"What is it you need to know?" My throat tightened against the wave of sympathy that washed over me. Unshed tears glistened in Pammy's eyes, and she blinked a couple of times in an effort to stop them from falling. I knew this because I did it all the time. Christmas commercials, articles in women's magazines, videos of soldiers coming home to their dogs—yeah, those really got me. "Maybe we can help you."

"I need to know how I died." She wiped her nose with the back of her hand, which, in my opinion, was gross whether a person was living or dead. "I want to know who killed me."

Now we were getting somewhere. If she could tell us something about her death, we might know where Parker would appear tonight.

"What do you remember?" Nate asked.

"Not much, really." She sniffed again and floated toward us. "Everybody had left for the night and I was on stage practicing my lines." A smile split her face. "Earlier that day Mr. Parker had told me I'd be going on for Miss Turner." Clasping her hands under her chin, she pressed her arms tightly to her body and swayed from side to side. "Me, the star of the show, I could barely believe it."

"That's wonderful, Pammy." I matched her excitement, but that suspicion I got when something was off nagged at me. "Did he say why Miss Turner wouldn't be acting that night?"

"No." As if that question had never crossed her mind, Pammy's expression softened to confusion. "All he said was that Miss Turner was indisposed for the evening."

"Indisposed how?" I asked.

Her lip curled into a pout. "I don't know. He just said indisposed, and I didn't ask. I was too excited about being bumped up to the starring role."

Samuel Parker had a real Ted Bundy vibe going on. From the way the two women spoke about him, he'd charmed his way into everybody's good graces, and nobody suspected he was a psycho killer. Pammy's story sounded more like a setup to me. Tell her she'd be the leading lady, lure her to the theater that night, and then murder her. My gaze flashed a silent question to Nate. He nodded in agreement.

"Can you tell us anything else about the night you died?" Nate's tone, though friendly and calm, had shifted into hunter mode. Where I kind of floundered my way through reaps, going on gut instinct and emotion, he collected information and categorized it. Watching him now, I was fairly certain he had two or three possible scenarios running through his head. "A sound or smell. The smallest detail might help us solve your murder."

"She'd come in earlier for a fitting," Arlene chimed in. "We had to alter all the outfits because Pammy was a size smaller than Miss Turner." A wicked smirk turned up her lip, and she gave a bark of laughter. "Boy, was she ever hot when I had to let the dresses back out."

"Carolyn was angry?" I asked. No woman liked to be reminded of her weight, especially an actress whose understudy was younger and thinner.

"Oh, yeah." Another raspy laugh woofed from Arlene. "Made quite a scene the next day, throwing clothes around the room, knocking over mannequins, screaming about being betrayed. She even got angry over the police shutting down the theater to investigate Pammy's murder. She scared the younger seamstresses half to death, but she only made me angry." The ghost shook her head. "The woman was horrible. Never knew what Parker saw in her, anyway."

"She was so beautiful and glamorous," Pammy said, the dreamy gleam back in her eyes. "And talented."

"Talented?" Another snort erupted from Arlene. "The woman couldn't act her way out of a parking ticket." She jabbed her cigarette in Pammy's direction. "I bet that's why Mr. Parker moved you up to lead actress. He'd finally realized what a hack Carolyn Turner was."

"Oh, no." Hovering a few inches above the floor, Pammy drifted forward, again wringing her hands together. "She was the star. Not me."

"Sweetie, you could act circles around her. Everybody knew it." Arlene took a long tug on her cigarette and then blew out. "And so did Carolyn."

Silence filled the room while the younger ghost absorbed what her friend had said. Not sure what was going on inside her head, I waited for her to speak first. We needed these two, especially Pammy. Hopefully, she'd remember something that would help us reap Samuel Parker. Though Arlene seemed to think he'd finally realized the gem of an actress he had in Pammy, I was more of the mind that he'd lured her to the empty theater that night under the guise of fulfilling her dreams. With opening night looming, what actress wouldn't put in overtime? Plus, she'd been young and gullible. Murder had probably been the last thing on Pammy's mind the night she was killed.

She snuffled again, breaking the hush in the room. "I didn't even get to perform."

My heart went out to her. "I'm sorry." The gown I still wore swished along the floor when I edged toward her. "We can't turn back time, but we can help you figure out who killed you." Stopping a few feet away, I held out my arms and smiled. "And afterward, we can help you cross over. I bet there's a big stage on the other side just waiting for you."

"Yeah?" she asked.

"Yeah." Once a spirit passed, I had no idea what happened to them, but if anybody deserved happiness in the afterlife, it was Pammy. "So…" I said, making a full circle back to Nate's previous question. "Can you remember anything at all about that night?"

Her translucent body paced back and forth in front of me. At least, I assumed she was pacing, but everything below her knees was transparent. "I was on stage practicing my lines." She stopped and closed her eyes. "The only lights were the spotlights, and I couldn't see much beyond the orchestra pit." Her eyes popped open. "Cologne. The kind Mr. Parker wore. I smelled it right before someone choked the life out of me."

"Well—" Again I glanced at Nate. "That seems a bit incriminating."

"Just a little." He straightened and stood. "Did you see who strangled you, Pammy? Or maybe got a glimpse of their hands or shoes?"

"No." Again she wrapped her hands protectively around her neck. "I was so panicked all I could think about was trying to get a breath. One minute I was clutching at the wire around my neck and the next…" Taking a deep breath, she hesitated. "I woke up dead."

There are spirits that deserve to be dead, either for being violent or stupid. Not Pammy. She'd deserved a happy life. Instead, she'd spent nearly seventy years haunting the old theater, trying to find out who killed her. When I moved to stand in front of her, she didn't retreat. It appeared we were finally building trust.

I gripped her shoulders, which was a perk of being a grim reaper. "We're going to help you figure this out."

"See, honey," Arlene said behind me. "I told you everything would work out."

"Arlene is right, so don't worry, okay?" I said, adding an extra dose of *I knew what the hell I was doing.*

She nodded. "Okay."

"You guys stay here," Nate said, moving toward the door. "I'm going to do a sweep of the stage."

I released the ghost and followed him. "Should I come?"

"No." His eyes darted from Pammy to me. "Stay here and see if you can get her to remember anything."

"What about not leaving me alone?" Crossing my arms over my chest, I leveled a stare at him and spoke through gritted teeth. "You know, the whole killing me thing?"

He glanced at his watch and back to me. "It's only seven o'clock. From what we've learned, I doubt he'll make an appearance before midnight. But just in case, stay here." He pulled open the door. "I won't be long."

Sometimes my life is too weird for even me to believe. This was one of those times. The door clicked shut behind Nate and I slowly turned back to the room and its occupants. "I guess it's just the three of us now."

Arlene lifted the cigarette, then slipped it between her lips, and sucked on the end. The damn thing was like something from the adult version of Willy Wonka's Chocolate Factory. The Never-ending Cigarette. What I wish I had right now was the never-ending wine bottle. When I died, that's what I was going to wish for in the afterlife, an Unemptying Wine Bottle that never went dry—and yoga pants that made me look like Heidi Klum. Pammy continued to hover in the corner, but at least she was smiling.

Stop a serial killer, solve a murder, don't get killed, yep, that about summed up my life.

CHAPTER FIVE

"Do you have a favorite costume, Pammy?" I asked, trying to stimulate conversation.

"Oh, yes." She floated forward and stopped at a small rack sitting away from the other wardrobe. Her hand drifted over the dusty white cloth bag hanging on the end. "I never got a chance to wear it, but I'd always hoped I would."

"What is it?" Not sure the ghost could heft the bulky bag, I lifted the garment. "It's heavy." I pulled the black zipper down and around the cover. The front flap peeled away to reveal a red and gold velvet gown. "Wow, that is beautiful."

"My best work." Arlene drifted forward, stopped, and rested her crossed arms over her round stomach, a smile tugging at her lips. "It was for Romeo and Juliet, but Mr. Parker scrapped the play after Pammy died."

"Was that the play you were supposed to perform in?" I asked.

"Yes." Her hand caressed the puffy sleeve, her gaze distant and wistful. "I was going to play Juliet, and Mikey Horn was going to play Romeo." The ghost gave a deep longing sigh. "He's so dreamy."

"I agree that Mikey is a good-looking kid," Arlene said, "But sweetie, I'm pretty sure he bats for the other team."

Pammy's face scrunched up in confusion. "I don't think Mikey ever played baseball."

"What I mean is, if Mikey had his choice, the play would be called Romeo and Julian." Arlene took a long tug on her cigarette and then blew out. "Understand?"

The actress's eyes narrowed. "Huh?"

"He's gay," I blurted. Hopefully, my bluntness wouldn't offend her mid-century sensibilities. "He likes guys." When she continued to stare at me, I added, "Like likes. Get it?"

"Oh yeah." She smiled sheepishly and waved my statement away. "I know, but maybe he hasn't met the right woman yet."

"As long as the woman is a man, then yeah," I said.

A raspy laugh ground from the seamstress. "Good one."

"It's possible, negative Nelly." Pammy continued glowering at her friend. "Anyway, I guess I'll never know what it feels like to play Juliet."

One of these days I'd learn to keep my mouth shut, but today wasn't the day. Her look of desolation and yearning badgered me to make a colossal suggestion. "Why don't you put on Romeo and Juliet here?"

"Oh no, I couldn't do that." The ghost's head shook violently. "Besides, tonight is Miss Turner's Midnight Spectacular."

"What is that?" I rehung the gown and zipped the bag.

"Every Halloween Miss Turner performs a one-woman play she wrote about being a young starlet in Hollywood." She sighed. "It's wonderful."

"Performs is a strong verb for what she does to that role." As if she had a bad taste in her mouth, Arlene smacked her lips a couple of times. "More like hacked it to pieces."

"Anywayyyyy..." Pammy shot the older woman a look of disapproval. "Everybody buys tickets to the Midnight Spectacular, so what's the point?"

"The point is," Arlene said, cutting me off, "It doesn't matter what play is being performed, just that something *is* showing. I guarantee they'd rather watch you as Juliet than sit through seven acts of Carolyn Turner's pretentious attempt at playing a naïve farm girl in Hollywood."

"Do you really think so?"

"Of course," I chimed in. Maybe putting on Romeo and Juliet would keep everybody occupied, plus, draw Samuel Parker out of the shadows. "There's probably a lot to do before midnight."

"First of all, we need to round up the other actors." Arlene swirled away from us and glided across the room. "They'll all need to be fitted."

"I'll go find Mikey." Clapping her hands, Pammy bounced up and down, emitting a high-pitched squeal. "He'll be so excited.

"And tell the other actors, too," the seamstress admonished, "Right? Not just Mikey."

"Of course, I'll ask the others." Before disappearing through the wall, she gave Arlene and I a gigantic grin. "But, Mikey first."

Without slowing her glide, the young ghost melted through the barrier, leaving me alone with Arlene.

"That's a handy trick," I said.

"Dopey broad." Shaking her head, Arlene rifled through the racks of costumes. "Bless her innocent heart."

"I'm going to change clothes." I had no idea what it took to put on a play, but with my luck, I'd somehow get dragged into doing the heavy lifting. Best to make myself scarce before somebody found a job for me. "After that, I'm going to find Nate."

"Didn't Mr. Nate say you should wait here?"

"Yeah, well, I don't always do what Mr. Nate says." I plastered on a reassuring smile. Midnight was still hours away, and it was probably still safe to walk around the theater alone. "Much to his dismay."

She gave me a worried look—well—maybe her expression waned on the side of ambiguous boredom more than worry. "Whatever you say, doll." A pile of velvets and brocades amassed in the center of a long table as she sorted the costumes. "I'll be here doing what I do best."

"Roger that." I stepped behind the screen and stripped out of the blue gown, climbing back into my reliable reaperwear. "I'll check back in a bit." I walked to the door and gripped the handle. "Break a leg."

Arlene's barking laughter followed me out the door. Unable to help myself, I smiled. She might be a gruff old bird, but her curt personality warmed a part of me reserved for stand-up comedians and crotchety old men.

Once in the hallway, I glanced at my watch. Where was Nate? He'd been gone way longer than it took to investigate the stage area. My stomach tightened against the idea of walking through the theater alone, but I needed to make sure he was all right. After all, facing harrowing circumstances was part of the partner code. Well, actually it wasn't. I made that up. Clearly, we didn't have a partner code since he wouldn't even high-five me, but, once we were finished with this job, I was definitely going to create one. Mainly because I was usually the one in trouble.

My boots clicked against the black and white tile squares of the floor as I moved down the corridor. I passed the first room on the right. The door stood open, but it was dark inside, making it impossible to see more than a foot into the room. I picked up my pace and shuffled past.

"Pssst."

The sound hissed from behind me and I whirled, striking a ninja pose, but nobody was there. I waited. "Hello?"

"Pssst," the voice came again. "In here."

Right, like I was going to fall for that again. "I don't think so." In case something or someone planned on flying out of the darkness at me, I inched backward. "Who's there?"

Fear wasn't a rational thing. I was a grim reaper and could manhandle just about any spirit and deliver them to my porter, but right now all I wanted to do was turn tail and run.

The faint image of a woman wavered inside the

doorway. Even before she'd fully formed, the frizzy hair and gigantic glasses gave her away. Evelyn Git.

I relaxed my stance and straightened, lowering my arms. "Hello."

The ghost solidified. She rested her shoulder against the doorframe. "I heard what you said in there, about the performance."

My mind hadn't quite caught up to the situation. "Performance?"

"Yeah, yeah." She swooped her hand in a circle. "You know, the kid playing Juliet." Her chin lowered, and she stared at me through the dark line of the brown gradient tint of her glasses. "I want in."

Evelyn didn't strike me as the actress type, especially as an Elizabethan performer. "You want a part in the play?"

"Jesus, no." She drifted toward me, her hands gesturing with each word she spoke. The hint of a New York accent laced her words, and with her dark Jackie O glasses and large gold hoop earrings, she looked like she stepped right off the page of a 1970s celebrity magazine. "I'm a society girl. I've got connections and can make this play huge."

"Okay." I'm not sure how I'd become the go-to

person for the production, but it was par for the course. "Knock yourself out."

"Excellent." She smiled, gesturing with her hands. "It's been so long since I've seen any action."

No time like the present to collect some info. "Evelyn Git—" I pointed at her. "Right?"

"You've heard of me?" When she smiled, her eyes widened and deep lines creased the corners of her mouth. She pressed her boney fingers against her chest. "How delightful."

"Who hasn't heard of Evelyn Git?" I said, playing on the ghost's ego. "Anchorage socialite, onetime owner of the City Center Theater, a woman ahead of her time."

"I was, wasn't I?" Propping her fists on her hips, she continued. "Those were the days. Parties, drugs, booze." She gave a contented sigh. "Good times." Her smile faded, and she lifted her shoulders in a single shrug. "Then I died."

"Yeah, I remember reading about that. I'm really sorry."

"Thank you, that's nice of you to say." She shrugged again. "What are ya gonna do? Everybody dies."

"Do you recall what happened that night, Evelyn? If I remember right, it was during your annual Halloween party."

"Was it ever?" The smile popped back on her face. "I'd had parties at the theater before, but that one was by far the best." She closed the distance between us, stopping about a foot away. It was far enough that she didn't hit me with her hand gestures when she spoke, but too close for personal comfort. "It was the grandest costume party Anchorage had ever seen. I mean people put some serious effort into their get-ups."

"It sounds wonderful." After her hand narrowly missed slicing through my arm, I eased back a few inches. When reaping, I use what's called *intent*. I can capture and hold on to a spirit. But if I'm not reaping, ghosts usually pass right through me, which feels like an icy blade cutting into my skin. Not fun, so I avoid casual contact as much as possible. "And the theater, did you have that all decorated?"

"Of course. I'd gone all out and hired a company out of Seattle to come up. They did everything from decorations to catering." She lifted her arms in a kind of jazz hands pose, and her voice lengthened into a singsong note. "Faaaabulous."

"So...what happened?" I gave her a tight but sympathetic smile. "Do you remember how you died?"

Her exuberance dissolved into a conspiratorial

whisper and she leaned toward me. "A ghost."

I hadn't expected such a concise answer. "Really?"

"Yep. A real live ghost."

Her comment hit me as ironic. One, because ghosts weren't alive. As a matter of fact, they are the opposite. And two, because she herself was a ghost, but I withheld my observation. "Did you see him when he killed you?"

"No." She frowned and crossed her arms over her chest. "But earlier that night, before I was murdered, I'd been flirting with a very handsome gentleman ghost."

It had to be Samuel Parker. The fact that Evelyn was killed a few hours later would be too much of a coincidence for it not to be him. "What did he look like?"

"Black hair, dark eyes."

Hands that fit nicely around your neck? It sure sounded like Parker from her vague description. "So, you actually spoke to him?"

"Oh yes." The fingers of her right hand caressed her neck and she sighed. "He told me he had been the original owner of the building and was happy it was being used again. I assured him of my plans to reopen the theater which seemed to make him happy."

"I bet." Then he'd have a fresh supply of blondes to choose from when the murdering mood struck. "Evelyn, do you think he was the one that murdered you?"

Her eyes rounded. "Good God, no. He was too polite and good looking to be a killer."

What was it with these female spirits? Just because a person was polite and handsome didn't mean he wouldn't take the first chance to strangle them. "Was there another ghost?"

"Tons." Her hands swooped up in an arc. "They were all over the theater. Like I said, best Halloween party ever." She lowered her hands and crossed her arms again. "But I never saw who murdered me. Choked me from behind with some kind of a wire." She snapped her fingers. "I was gone like that."

Most spirits seemed to have a cavalier attitude about their deaths. A lot of them talked about their demise as if it happened to somebody else. What I'd learned since becoming a reaper was that being dead was a lot like being alive, business as usual. How they died was what scared people most. Strangulation was not high on my best ways to die list.

"Anything else you remember? Perfume? Did you see the killer's hands or shoes?"

"No, but then again, I was blotto by that time." She paused and tapped her index finger against her lip. "It was exactly midnight. I remember hearing the clock in the foyer chime." Her arms lowered, her shoulders sagging. "I never realized that before."

Weird. Pammy was killed around midnight too. It seemed Parker had a whole *murder at midnight* thing going on. "Maybe tonight we'll be able to figure out who's responsible for your death."

"I don't care who did it." She waved a hand at me. "What's done is done."

"If you don't want to know who murdered you, why are you still hanging around the theater?" Normally, unfinished business kept spirits tied to the physical realm.

"I like the people." She flung her arms wide. "Heaven couldn't possibly have a better party than what's right here."

"So, you haven't crossed over because you like to party, not because of unfinished business?"

"The only unfinished business I had was a night of passion with a couple of the band members from the Rolling Stones. Got interrupted by the police for noise complaints." A wicked smile quirked up the corners of her mouth. "Doesn't matter, they'll all be dead eventually, and maybe we'll finish what we started."

"Thanks for the visual," I said against the urge to

gag. "Okay then, I guess you have a performance to prep for." More than likely she didn't have any more information that would help us with Parker, and I was getting antsy about finding Nate. "So, I'll leave you to it."

"You won't be sorry." Her image faded. "This is going to be a night to remember."

I had no doubt of that. When she'd completely disappeared, I pivoted and started down the hall. My mind sifted through everything each ghost had told me. The nagging feeling in my gut prodded me again. Something about Samuel Parker didn't add up. If he truly had been a serial killer, why would he have murdered Evelyn Git? She'd said he'd been thrilled about the theater reopening. Even if the reason he'd been happy was the new supply of blondes, he'd have to murder, it didn't make sense for him to kill the one person who could make that happen for him.

Giving myself a mental shake, I pushed aside my doubts. No matter, we had to reap him—and any other spirit we could get our hands on.

CHAPTER SIX

The torchlight to my left flickered as I passed, and my step slowed. I'd been so caught up with everything happening around me, I hadn't given much thought to being alone in the theater again. Chills skittered up my spine and along my arms. With the increased paranormal activity tonight, there was no guarantee Parker wasn't already stalking me.

Having thoroughly freaked myself out with that thought, I unhooked the black cylinder from my waist and twisted the ornately carved ring. The whisper of the handle elongating hissed, and the smoky blade of the scythe formed at the tip. I won't lie, the thing was so awesome that I sometimes played with it at home after the kids left for school. Hal, my porter, and grandfather, had given me the scythe after my adventure in Las Vegas. There were less than a hundred in existence, and my sweet baby was the first—Death's original scythe. So stinkin' cool.

Feeling more confident now that I had the ultimate weapon of death at the ready, I advanced quickly down the hall. Brilliant lights illuminated the stage, but it was empty. "Nate?" My whispered call reverberated back to me, and then silence. "Nate?"

Still nothing.

Crap.

My heartbeat quickened, the need to find him pressing me forward. Taking the stairs to the left, I climbed down to the house floor and stopped, letting my eyes adjust to the dark interior beyond the lights.

"Ticket?"

"Ahhh!" I gasped and spun toward the deep drawl behind me, my scythe at the ready. The spirit of an old man hovered an inch inside my personal bubble, his white-gloved hand extending even farther into my comfort zone. I took an exaggerated step backward. "Excuse me?"

"Ticket?" When he spoke, his jowls wobbled. His half-closed eyes made it tough to determine if he stared at my face or my knees. "May I have your ticket, please?"

"I…uhhh…" Holding my scythe with one hand, I patted my pants pocket with the other. "I seemed to have misplaced it."

"Misplaced it?" said someone from behind me.

"Holy crap." I pivoted again and faced a small, much younger man, maybe in his forties. The way his head shook from side to side, his nose pointing in the air as if smelling my breath, reminded me of a ferret. "You guys just keep popping up, don't you?"

"Sorry." His clipped apology didn't sound

convincing. He hooked his thumbs in the pockets of his vest and pursed his lips at me. "Ma'am, did I hear you say you don't have a ticket?"

"Yeah, I must have misplaced it." Movement across the theater caught my attention. Yet another gossamer ghost dressed in the same black suit and white gloves floated up the aisle. Maybe it was a Halloween thing, but the paranormal activity in the theater seemed to be ramping up even faster than I'd originally thought. "Actually, I'm here with a friend. Tall guy, brownish-blond hair, amazing blue eyes. You haven't seen him by chance, have you?"

"No, ma'am, I have not. You're the only *corporeal* I've come across." He said *corporeal* as if it was a dirty word. Continuing to block my path, he scowled at me. "I have to ask you to vacate the theater if you don't have a ticket."

"How about I buy a ticket?" That seemed the quickest solution to the problem.

"Can't," he countered. "The show is sold out."

"How can that be?"

"It's Halloween night. The only performance of the year." He stepped back and indicated that I should leave. "I'll escort you out."

"I'm not going anywhere until I find my partner." I

lowered my scythe and held it horizontally in front of me. His eyes darted to the weapon, but other than that, he didn't flinch. "Do you know who I am?"

"I couldn't care less, ma'am. The only thing that matters is whether you have a ticket or not."

The guy really took his job seriously. *OCD much?* "How about we make a deal?" I planted the handle of my scythe next to his foot and straightened my spine, trying to look as imposing as possible. "You forget that my partner and I don't have tickets, and I won't send your soul to the bowels of Hell."

His lips pinched so tight I thought his jaw might crack. The loud inhalation through his nose left no doubt that he wasn't thrilled about the choice I'd given him. For a couple of seconds, he didn't say anything, and I got a little nervous that I might actually have to reap this joker. Then I'd have to have Hal take him for a trip around the circles of Hell before depositing him where he belonged—just to prove my point.

"Fine." His nostrils flared a couple of times and his mouth only relaxed a fraction. "I'll add you to the roster." With that, he turned and marched up the aisle.

"You do that," I called after him. Some people—give them a little authority and they think they run the world. I glared at his back and mumbled, "And I'll tell Hell to keep your seat warm."

Having secured our theater passes, I scanned the house floor again. Another usher spirit drifted along the balcony level, and a couple of ghosts had claimed their seats for the upcoming performance, but still no Nate. Maybe arriving spirits had waylaid him like the ferret-guy's ghost had held me up.

I made my way into the outer lobby, but it was empty. Something seemed different. The gold gleamed brighter, and the crystals on the chandelier sparkled as if they were no longer covered in decades of dust. Even the rose-colored carpet didn't seem so faded. Maybe more than just the spirits came back to life on Halloween. Maybe it was the whole damn theater.

"Nate!" Stealth no longer seemed necessary since every ghost in the place knew we were there. "Nate!"

Soft whispers sounded to my right. My head snapped toward the noise, hoping it was him. Instead of my partner, I saw a soft yellow glow. I tensed, my scythe held in a ready-to-reap position. The light pulsed a few times before materializing into a spirit.

She had white blond hair and big blue eyes. Ginormous diamonds winked at her neck just above her enviable bosom, and I knew the spirit had to be Carolyn Turner. She held out a pink-gloved hand and whispered, "Help me."

"Carolyn?" Jackpot. If I could get ahold of her, she might be able to tell us more about Parker—or—maybe we could lure him to us. Of course, using her as bait wouldn't be our first plan, but I wouldn't stop her if she volunteered. We needed to take this serial killing jackass out of commission for good, and she might be our ace in the hole.

"I can help you."

I'd only moved a foot toward the ghost when another spirit appeared between us. The breath jammed to a stop in my throat and I froze. Samuel Parker. Before my brain jumpstarted back to reaper-mode, he whirled toward me and extended his arms. From his expression, he had every intention of choking me.

Rational thought refused to kick in, completely forgetting the fact that I held the scythe, or that I'd been trained to reap the worst kind of spirits. Nope, the only thought racing through my mind was, *RUN!*

I stumbled backward with no clear plan as to where I was going, or what I would do when he caught me. A loud shriek suddenly split the quiet. I confess—it was me. I totally scream like the popular cheerleader in a horror movie seconds before she's killed.

With his arms straight out in front of him, his fingers spread, Parker closed the distance between us, his eyes dark and focused. Even when I tripped over the handle of my scythe, it didn't register to use the weapon.

My idiocy could have meant my end if it hadn't been for Nate. Out of nowhere, he launched himself at the ghost and connected with Parker. The two men crashed to the floor, toppling head-over-heels until coming to a stop a couple of yards away from me.

Maybe it was because Nate's life was in danger now and not mine, but sense finally kicked in. I jumped to my feet, howling with a battle cry Conan the Barbarian would have been proud of and bolted toward them. Parker sat on top of Nate with his hands pinning Nate's shoulders to the ground. When the ghost heard my yell, his head snapped up. Our eyes locked for a fraction of a second. With one look at my face, he no doubt thought it unwise to go head-to-head with a crazy, scythe-wielding wackjob. In one smooth move, he jumped up and sped toward the closest wall. Unfortunately, Nate still had ahold of Parker when the ghost passed through the solid barrier.

The very act of my partner slamming into the wall was a horrifically awesome sight. For a few seconds, it looked as if someone had hung him like a painting. One arm and both legs dangled limply, while the other arm remained somewhere underneath his body. Then, like a cannonball, he fell to the floor, unconscious.

"Nate." I practically flew across the room, forgetting about Parker or Carolyn Turner. "Nate, can you hear me?" I dropped to the floor next to him and pressed my fingers to his neck to make sure he wasn't dead. A strong beat pulsed against my touch. "Thank God."

Despite what my junior high babysitting CPR course had advised about moving someone with a possible head or neck injury, I gently rolled Nate onto his back. A spot on his forehead purpled and swelled, as did an area on his left cheek. A major headache loomed in his near future—if I could get him to wake up.

"I haven't seen a collision like that since Iditarod Doris slammed Black Betty into the wall at the Northern Lights Roller Derby Finals," said a man above me.

Cradling Nate's head on my lap, I craned my neck to see the speaker. A young man leaned over the counter and smiled down at me. He wore a black suit like the ushers in the theater, but the neck appeared to be a couple of sizes too big. "Excuse me?"

"Your friend, he hit that wall just like Black Betty

did in the roller derby finals of fifty-eight." He gave me a wide, gap-toothed grin. "But she had a helmet on, so she didn't get knocked out. Broke her arm though."

"Fascinating." I turned my attention back to Nate and stroked his forehead, but avoided the purple goose egg. "Can you hear me, Nate?"

A low groan emanated from him, and relief swept through me. Maybe I should have called the ambulance, or at the very least found some ice to put on his head. Why hadn't I had the foresight to pack a cooler? Then I'd have an ice pack or a can of cold soda to lay against his bruises. At that point, I would have settled for a cold ham sandwich.

"What happened to him?" The spirit of a woman glided toward us and stopped on the opposite side of Nate. Decked out in a short red velvet and gold dress, she swung the tray that hung around her neck to the side and stared down at us. Red curls corkscrewed from under her gold pillbox hat, and her big brown eyes roamed up and down his body before shifting to me. "Is he drunk?"

"No, he ain't drunk, Ginger," The concession guys said, "Mr. Parker nearly dragged him through the wall."

"Jeepers!" Her thick black lashes fluttered rapidly and her mouth puckered into a cupid bow. "Why'd he go and do that?"

Explaining that we were grim reapers, there to send their boss to the afterlife, seemed a bit above their pay grade and intelligence level. "You wouldn't happen to have any ice on that tray, would you, Ginger?"

She shook her head and knelt. "Sorry, just cigarettes and chewing gum."

My gaze flashed to her hands. "Hey, can you press your hand against his forehead?"

"Huh?"

"Right here." I pointed to the burgeoning lump. "Just lay your hand over the top."

"Sure, I guess." After lifting the tray from around her neck and depositing it on the floor, the ghost repositioned herself. "Will I hurt him?"

"Don't worry about that." I smiled at her. "I doubt he'll feel a thing."

The theory that cold spots were ghosts is true. It's even more so for grim reapers. Sometimes being touched by a spirit feels like an icicle slicing through my flesh, especially if the ghost is violent. Other times, when a spirit is gentle or calm, the connection is merely cold, and that's exactly what I needed from Ginger right now.

She settled her right hand over Nate's forehead, and her mouth turned upward in an uncertain smile. "Like this?"

"Perfect," I said in a reassuring tone. Nate groaned again and rolled his head toward the ghost. "I think he's coming out of it." I rested my hand on his chest and leaned over him. "Open your eyes, Nate." His eyelids cracked open and slowly widened. I could tell his gaze was unfocused, so I shifted and placed my face directly above his. "How are you feeling?"

"Like I was hit by a train." His eyelids drifted shut again. "Did I get him?"

"If by get you mean practically taking out a wall with your head," the concession guy said, "then yeah, buddy, you got him good."

I frowned at the ghost and then returned my attention to Nate. "Sorry, he got away."

"Damn." His stare drifted upward and settled on Ginger.

She smiled at him. "Hello."

"I must have hit that wall pretty hard." His gaze remained fixed on the beautiful ghost.

"You sure did," Ginger said. The hand she covered his forehead with slid lower to gently brush the area above his eyebrows. "Your lady-friend had me put my hand on your forehead." Her expression relaxed into a smile. "I must have a magic touch because you're awake."

The urge to push her hand off his head shoved at me. I told her to cover his bruise, not soothe his brow. Instead, I asked, "Can you sit up?"

"Maybe." With my help, he shifted and rolled to a sitting position, grunting with obvious discomfort on his ascent. "Remind me to let go next time."

"Seriously? You're actually going to need reminding after that impact?" What I wanted to tell him was that there wasn't going to be a next time, but we were reapers, and his clients were violent criminals. Thinking he'd—we'd—never be in a situation like this again would be foolish. "Didn't the wall drive that point home?"

"You'd think so." He extended his arm, silently asking for help to stand.

Wedging my shoulder under his body, we slowly stood. "Maybe we should go to the hospital and get you checked out just to make sure you don't have any internal damage." We limped to the concession counter, and Nate braced his arm against the edge. "We could come back when they give you the *all clear.*

"There's no time." He shook his head. "Parker is already here. The sooner we get him taken care of the better."

"You know if you'd been killed, I would have had to reap you, right?" I furrowed my brow, because I didn't know how to do that cool arching thing, and peered down my nose at him. "Because that was stupid with a capital s."

"I get it. Not my finest hour, but I wouldn't have had to tackle him if you'd stayed in the dressing room."

"If you'd come back in a reasonable amount of time, I wouldn't have had to come looking for you," I retorted.

He straightened, wobbled a bit, but caught hold of the counter and steadied himself. "Let me sit for a few minutes and then I'll be ready to go."

Stubborn, another s-word that described him. We'd done this dance before, during other tough reaps, and I knew I had a better chance of playing Juliet than I did getting Nate to go to the hospital. I turned to Ginger. "Is there somewhere he can sit down that's out of the way?"

"Sure, there are a couple of rooms over here." She pointed to the end of the foyer and glided toward the first door. We can use one of these. Nobody ever goes in there anymore."

"Ginger!" The concession guy said, "Nobody's supposed to go back there except Mr. Parker and you know who." He floated through the counter stopping a few inches away from us. "He'll be really mad." His voice dropped to a whisper. "And so will she."

"So will who?" I asked. If there was another ghost involved, we needed to know about it.

"Miss Turner." Ginger shook her head, her curls violently bouncing. "She didn't like anybody going into her sitting room." Screwing her face up with determination, she glared at her coworker. "But I don't care." Spinning away from us, she continued her course toward the room. "This is an emergency and I plan on helping. Why don't you go back to selling candy and beverages, Eddie?

"Fine." He backed away from us. "But, don't come crying to me when she starts yelling and throwing things."

Ginger harrumphed and then waved a dismissive hand in the air. "Don't listen to him. He's always been afraid of Miss Turner. Actually, he's afraid of most women." She drifted forward. "Eddie was right about one thing, though. She sure can yell."

After wrapping my arm around Nate's waist, I helped him toward the room. A lot seemed to happen behind the scenes at the theater, and Ginger appeared to have a bead on the gossip. That was good for us. Perhaps she knew something that could help us bring Samuel Parker down.

"We appreciate your assistance, Ginger," Nate said. "Maybe you can help us with our investigation."

Investigation, that was a nice way to describe what we were attempting.

"Help you?" she asked. "How?"

"Can you tell us anything about Mr. Parker?" Nate leaned heavily against me, his body connected to mine as we walked. The chance for full body contact didn't present itself very often. And I'll be honest, with my arm around his waist, and his around my shoulder, it was difficult to keep my train of thought on our current situation. "What kind of man was he?" he continued.

"Oh, Mr. Parker was wonderful," Ginger said, a dreamy smile spreading across her face. "He was the best boss, always worrying about the workers. He bought everybody gifts after each production. Not just the actors and stage crew, but even those of us who worked in the rest of the theater." A smile stretched her mouth, displaying perfectly white teeth. "And every Christmas, he threw a catered party with Santa Claus and everything."

"He sounds very generous." Nothing like the psychopathic murderer the file portrayed him to be. Then again, a lot of serial killers were like that. It made it easier to lure people into their trap, get them trusting, and then kill them when they weren't looking. "How about him and Miss Turner? What kind of relationship did they have?"

Her wistful smile evaporated, and her voice dropped to a whisper. "I know it's not a very kind thing to say." Her gaze darted up and down the hall. "But I didn't much care for Miss Turner. Working here was a lot of fun until she arrived. Acted like she owned the place, and I think that was her plan. She'd only been here a couple weeks before she had her hooks and Mr. Parker."

"Would you say their relationship was volatile?" Nate asked.

"Heck, yeah." The ghost stopped in front of a door with a giant gold star hanging on the front. "At first, they only fought a little, but the longer they were together, the worse it seemed to get. She didn't care where they were, or who was around. If she was angry, she let him know it."

"She sounds delightful," I said, lacing my comment with sarcasm. "Would you say he was a jealous type?"

"Mr. Parker?" She shook her head. "Not that I could tell. Miss Turner was the one that had the jealousy problem. Always yelling about him cheating on her, or that he looked at another woman, even if he was just being friendly to the patrons." She blew out a breath. "Anyway, this is her dressing room. You should be able to rest in here. She's got a real nice couch."

"Thank you." I turned the knob, and the door opened with a single squeak. I reached around and flipped on the light. "We really appreciate your help, Ginger. If you happen to see Miss Turner, could you please let me know?"

"Sure." She hitched her thumb over her shoulder. "Well, I need to get back to work. I wouldn't want to get in trouble, or worse yet, fired." With that, she turned and headed down the hall.

Nate unwound his arm from my shoulder and limped across the room. A low groan oozed from him when he lowered his body to the couch but that was the only complaint he made. "We need a plan."

"Everybody around here really liked Samuel Parker." I plopped onto the pink chair next to the couch. "Either he was one of the most charming serial killers that ever lived, or we have our story wrong."

"You don't think Parker was a serial killer?"

"I don't know." I leaned back, running my fingers through the sides of my hair, and then locked them on top of my head. "I can't shake this feeling that we're missing a big piece of the puzzle. Four women murdered, and yet nobody around here has said a single derogatory thing about Parker."

"If that's the case, then what is the missing piece?" Nate shifted and rested against the large rolled arm of the couch. "He had a motive."

"Did he?" The more I thought about Parker being the killer, the less it set well with me. "All the file said was that he killed four women. But the police report never gave him a motive." I held up my hand, ticking off the ideas that had been rambling around in my head since we started this investigation. "He's wealthy, successful, people loved him, handsome, and basically he had everything in the world to live for. Why kill himself?"

"Just because a person has all those things going for him doesn't mean he's not still a maniacal killer, or just plain crazy." His gaze narrowed on me. "Come on, Carron, you can't deny he was coming right for you."

"No, that's true." The memory was still fresh in my mind, and my hands instinctively went to my throat—just like Pammy's had when I mentioned her death. "There is no denying he had it in for me." I released my neck and rubbed my arms, trying to chase away the cold lingering fear. "You're probably right. I'm over thinking this." My doubts were starting to cloud my judgment. "We don't need to solve the crime. We just need to reap his soul."

"Exactly."

I sat forward. "So, what now?"

"We draw him out." Nate scrubbed his hands over his face and winced when he touched the purple bruise. "Damn!" He sucked in a sharp breath and gently fingered his cheek. "I'm going to enjoy paying back Samuel Parker."

"Okay, hero, but try not to get any more head trauma." I bound to my feet. "Crap! I forgot my scythe in the lobby. I'll be right back."

"Be careful." Sitting forward, he rested his elbows on his knees and leveled a stare at me. "Parker knows you're here. Now more than ever we need to stick together. Grab your scythe and come directly back."

I nodded. "I will."

"I mean it, Carron. Don't get sidetracked."

I snorted a laugh. "Like that would ever happen."

Before he could reply, I bolted out of the room. Yes, I had a tendency to follow the shiny object, but this was about my scythe. Nothing could distract me from getting my baby back.

The strange whisper I'd heard seconds before I'd seen Carolyn Turner in the lobby, sounded behind me. I stopped and slowly turned. Nope, nothing was going to distract me from retrieving my scythe, nothing…except for maybe the ghost of Carolyn Turner.

CHAPTER SEVEN

Her image hovered at the end of the hall, her hand extended again, beckoning me to her. But this time she didn't look so scared. I didn't move. No way was I going to chase after a ghost without my scythe. "Wait there." I held up my finger. "I'll be right back."

I pivoted and ran to the lobby which was pretty amazing considering there weren't a lot of things that could induce me to run. My scythe had compacted back into the cylinder and rested next to the concession counter.

"You're back." Eddie stopped polishing the mirrored surface. "Is it because you got in trouble?"

"Nope just forgot something." I snatched the black cylinder from the floor and re-hooked it to my belt loop. "No time to talk."

He called out something to my departing back, but I ignored him, not wanting to keep Carolyn Turner waiting. I sped past the dressing room and rounded the corner, skidding to a stop. My adrenaline rush dwindled. "Damn," I uttered to the empty corridor. "Miss Turner?" I inched my way down the hall, stopping to peer into the open rooms. "Miss Turner, are you here?"

No answer. Remembering Nate's warning, I gave

up the search and booked it back, pausing just outside the dressing room. Maybe Miss Turner had wanted to show me something in one of the rooms. That would be a good place to continue our search for Parker.

"Did you get it?" Nate called from inside.

"Yeah." After taking one last look down the hall, I stepped inside and patted the cylinder. "It was right where I left it."

"At least something went right tonight." Nate pushed to his feet. "We need to get moving. We're running out of time."

"Are you sure you're up for it?" He seemed steady on his feet and the glazed look in his gaze had been replaced by determination. Poor Parker, the ghost had no idea what he was in for when Nate got ahold of him. "We can afford a couple more minutes."

"I'm tired of sitting." He headed toward the door. "Let's check out the rooms down this hallway."

"About that." I hesitated. "I just saw Carolyn Turner again—at the end of the hall."

His eyebrows lifted, and he smiled. "That must've been hard, Carron."

Even though I was fairly certain I wouldn't like his answer, I stilled myself and asked. "What was hard?"

"Deciding to retrieve your scythe instead of chasing her ghost."

"You have no idea. If it had been anything besides my scythe, I would've chased her down. Even that big ass bag of Halloween candy would have taken a backseat to finding out what Carolyn Turner wanted."

"Wow, ghost over junk food." His smile spread. "It's good to know you can exercise common sense when needed."

"Don't bank on that. I could go rogue at any second depending on my blood sugar level or time of the month."

"Too much information. But good to know."

Figuring he neither needed nor wanted my help, I pushed past him and took the lead. Once in the hallway, I pointed toward the end. "She was there."

"Did she say anything?"

"No, just did that creepy beckoning thing." My fingers stroked the cylinder hanging off my belt loop, while my other hand pressed the raven charm at my neck. Both gave me a measure of comfort, but I wasn't foolish enough to think I was one-hundred percent protected. "Let's start at the end and work our way back to the dressing room."

"That's as good of a plan as any, "Nate said.

"Do you want to lead, or should I?"

"I'll lead." Clearly still smarting from his dance with Parker and the wall, he shouldered past me.

Some of the doors were locked, while others stood open. The first thing I did at each room was flip on the lights. And when we left, I made no effort to shut them off again. Like I'd said, I hoped Lizzie Git had set aside extra money for utilities this month.

At the end of the hall stood a dark wood door. Ornate carvings curled around the inlaid rectangle, and a crystal and brass doorknob sparkled in the bright light. Thankfully the shut door was unlocked. Nate turned the handle and pushed it open. Of course, I reached around and flipped the light switch.

"This has to be Parker's office." I stepped over the threshold and into a room decorated for a man. Wainscoting, oversized desk chair, and desk, tall wooden file drawer. The whole place screamed manly hangout. My gaze scanned the room for any sign of Parker's ghost, but it appeared spirit-free. "There might be something here we can use to draw him out. Maybe this is what Carolyn Turner wanted to show me."

"Let's hope." Nate stopped and looked at me. "Do you feel that? It's cold in here."

"The whole theater is cold." The words died on my

tongue. He was right. Unlike the rest of the theater, the office felt several degrees cooler. "Okay, that's creepy."

"He probably hangs out here." Edging further into the room, Nate headed for the massive desk and pulled the chain on the brass desk lamp, illuminating the green glass shade. "I'll start here. You check out the rest of the room."

I nodded and moved toward a door at the opposite end of the office. It had the same glass knobs and details as the main office door but appeared narrower. On the other side, I found a sitting room. The furnishings were of high quality and matched the office decor. The same Wainscoting hugged the lower section of the walls, and two leather chairs sat angled in front of the stone fireplace. An Oriental rug that would have looked great in my living room spread out beneath the chairs, making the room quite cozy. Along the wall to my left, a table held an old fashion radio and dozens of silver picture frames. Floor to ceiling wooden bookshelves encased the far wall, and every space had been filled with books, books, and more books.

This must've been Parker's private sitting room. Away from the crowd and bustle of the theater life, he'd probably found peace here, or maybe this was where he plotted his next murder.

I stopped in front of the table and picked up a silver

picture frame embellished with flowers and crystals. Though the woman in the picture was much younger than the previous photograph I'd seen, I recognized her.

"Her name was Irene," said a voice behind me.

At the sound of the intruder, the picture frame nearly slipped from my fingers. My head snapped in the direction of the fireplace. Samuel casually leaned against the mantle, appearing very relaxed. To my relief, his menacing expression was gone, and he no longer looked as if he wanted to kill me. Now, he resembled the Samuel Parker everybody had described, charming, handsome, and I could see how easily a woman could be fooled by his laid back nature. Not me. I'd seen his dark side.

Wanting to free up my hands, I set the picture back on the table and then turned to face him fully. "She was your sister, well, stepsister, right?"

"I always considered her to be my sister." He toyed with the fringe dangling from the mantel runner. His voice took on a reflective tone. "I miss her very much."

What I wanted to say was, "Then, maybe you shouldn't have murdered her." But common sense won out. Instead, I nodded sympathetically. I wanted to alert Nate, but I didn't want to scare off Parker. Besides our little encounter in the lobby, this was the first time we'd actually come face-to-face with his spirit.

"I'm sorry for your loss." If I could keep him talking, maybe Nate would make his way to the room and figure out what was going on. "She was very beautiful."

"Yes, she was," he said, lowering his arm and peering directly at me. "You kind of remind me of her, actually."

"Me?" I glanced at the picture and then back to him. "Do you really think so?" Again, my eyes darted from the picture to the ghost. The last thing I wanted was for him to start comparing me to his dead sister. I scrunched up my face. "I don't see the resemblance."

"Around here." He circled his finger, indicating his eye area. "She had the same shade of eyes as you."

My fingers toyed with the black cylinder at my belt. In a matter of seconds, I could have the scythe out and extended. Hopefully, I was faster than him, but first, I needed to unhook it from my belt loop without him noticing. I slipped my finger under the latch, preparing to detach it. With two words he stopped me.

"Please don't." Holding his hand out in front of him, he stayed my action. "I know what that is, and I know who you are."

I lowered my hand. "Well, if you know who we are,

you must know why we're here."

"Yes." His expression softened and the tension around his eyes relaxed. His gaze pleaded with me not to release my scythe, yet at the same time, he seemed resigned to his fate. "I can't let you take me. At least not yet. And, I can't let you near Carolyn."

Of course, he couldn't let us near Carolyn. The last thing he wanted was for us to help out one of his victims. In an effort to keep him talking, I asked, "Why not?"

"Because it wouldn't be in your best interest."

Not letting me speak with Carolyn wouldn't be in *his* best interest. His gaze traveled past me, and for a second I thought Nate had entered the room. Parker's expression darkened and narrowed. A low growl rumbled from him. It was like watching the transformation of Dr. Jekyll and Mr. Hyde.

"Come here." He floated toward me, his hands raised just like they'd been when he attacked me in the lobby. "Don't!"

Had that approach worked on all his victims? No way was I getting anywhere near him. Unable to stop myself, I took a step backward, intent on yelling for Nate. Before I could utter a sound, an icy vise slipped around my neck and squeezed.

I gasped and clawed at my throat, but there was nothing to latch onto, no fingers, no scarf, no rope. The pressure increased, preventing me from taking a full breath. The blood pounded in my ears and I thought I heard Samuel yelling, but the only thing I could focus on was breaking free of the choking hold and not passing out. When blackness invaded the edges of my vision, I lifted my foot and tried to kick my attacker, but my foot merely passed through the air, not connecting.

I couldn't breathe, and seconds before I passed out, Parker rushed toward me with his hands extended. My eyes squeezed shut in a feeble attempt to brace for impact. Shards of ice impaled me, slicing my body from front to back as Parker's spirit passed completely through me. Though the pain from his invasion lingered, sending tremors to the center of my bones, the pressure around my neck instantly vanished.

My knees buckled, and I stumbled backward, knocking into the table and toppling several of the picture frames to the ground. Like a rag doll, my body crumpled, landing on top of the broken glass from the picture frames. I gasped, sucking in a lungful of air, faintly aware of the cutting shards, but I couldn't force my body to move.

"Lisa!" Nate shouted from the doorway, at least I

think it was the doorway. At that moment, I was doing good just to be conscious. "Lisa! Can you hear me?"

"Yeah." The word came out raspy, and my throat throbbed. I braced my hands against the floor and pushed up, but collapsed again when a sharp pain shot through the palms of my hands. "Ouch!"

"Careful." Nate straddled me and scooped up my body. I'm not going to lie, even though I was in pain, I found the fact that he could lift me very sexy. "You're lying in glass." Shifting, he got us clear of the shards, and then lowered back to the floor, placing me in front of him. "What happened?"

"Samuel Parker." I watched Nate pick a triangular piece of glass out of my palm, liking the protective way he cared for me. "He showed up a few seconds after I came into the room. Said he knew who we were and why we were here."

"Did that make him mad? Is that why he attacked you?" His hold on my wrist tightened.

"No. He said he couldn't let us take him yet. He also said he couldn't let me near Carolyn Turner."

"Probably because he doesn't want her to be reaped. Then who would he torment?" He lifted the edge of his shirt and gently brushed the material across my palm. "He's even more dangerous than we thought."

"I don't think so." I sat back on my heels and pulled my hand from his grip. "I think he was warning me off, not threatening me."

"But he attacked you."

"No, I don't think he did. We were standing there talking and suddenly somebody started choking me from behind. It had to be a spirit because I couldn't see or feel their hands, and I couldn't pry their grip loose." I swallowed hard, the spit refusing to go down. "But, I think Parker saw whoever was behind me. He suddenly got all menacing and yelled. At first, I thought he was shouting at me, but when something started choking me, I realized he was talking to my attacker."

Reclaiming his hold on my arm, he pulled me toward him, and then cupped my cheeks between his hands. His eyes roamed my face, not romantically, but to check me out for cuts and bruises. "How did you get free?"

"Parker rushed the attacker and passed through me." Nate grimaced. "Yeah, it hurt like hell." My body gave an involuntary shudder. "But, whoever was choking me let go, and both spirits disappeared." Our eyes locked. Being only a couple of inches away from him, I could see the green flecks in his eyes, making me hyper-aware of his body heat. Gingerly touching my neck, I cleared my throat and sat back again, trying to put a little distance between us. At the moment, I was feeling very vulnerable and would have no problem letting him comfort me. "Then you found me."

He didn't look away. His mouth pulled into a straight line and his gaze narrowed. He was upset, and from the firm set of his jaw, he was having a hard time keeping it reined in." We need to finish up this job. It's getting too dangerous around here."

"I know this goes against everything we read in the file, but I don't think Samuel Parker murdered those women." I shook my head. "He saved me. That doesn't seem like the actions of a serial killer."

"If not Parker, who?" Nate pushed to his feet and then held out his hands to me. "From what you've told me, the only person who makes sense is Carolyn Turner."

I gripped his hands and let him pull me to my feet. Besides a couple of cuts from the glass and my sore neck, I was unhurt. "Yeah." My head bobbed up and down as the idea took root. "That's exactly who murdered those women. It makes a lot more sense for her to be the killer than Samuel Parker."

"A jealous lover?" He bent and picked up the

broken picture of Irene White. "Could it be that simple?"

"Nothing is ever that simple." Clearly, he knew nothing about women. "Never underestimate the amount of rage behind a woman's jealousy."

"That's a whole lot of rage. Especially if she murdered Parker's sister."

"Psychotic and jealous, a deadly combination." Being jealous enough to murder a person was completely foreign to me. Even when my husband and I were at the height of our relationship, I would have never contemplated killing another woman out of jealousy. Carolyn Turner was seriously crazy-pants nutso, and I'd stepped right into her sites just by talking to him for less than five minutes. "If Parker had shown a preference to Irene over Carolyn that would have made her angry. And it's no coincidence that Pammy was murdered the night before she was supposed to go on in Carolyn's place."

"Being replaced by the understudy…" Nate blew out a low whistle. "That had to piss her off."

"In her twisted mind, she probably thought if she got the sister and the understudy out of the way, she'd have Samuel all to herself." Personally, I'd never known anyone that irrational, but I'd seen them on the Internet. Sometimes, I wondered if the person was for real or just made up for the benefit of their audience. Unfortunately, it seemed Carolyn Turner was no fake. In life, she'd been a bona fide psychopath, and it looked like she'd carried that lovely trait into the afterlife. "Didn't work though."

"The one question I have," Nate said, "is why Evelyn Git? Parker and Turner were dead by the time Evelyn hosted her Halloween party."

"Because," I said, feeling rather superior that I had information he didn't. "Evelyn had contact with Samuel during her party. Carolyn must have seen them talking, got jealous, and killed Evelyn." The pieces started to fall into place, the gnawing doubt I'd had since we started this case abating. Things were finally making sense. "Evelyn told me that Parker had been ecstatic about her reopening the theater."

Nate crossed his arms over his chest and scowled at me. "When did you talk to Evelyn Git?"

"A few minutes before you got up close and personal with the wall." I smiled sweetly. "Even when she told me about her encounter with him, it hadn't made sense that Parker murdered her. She was doing exactly what he wanted her to do."

"You might be right. All this time we've been hunting for Parker when we should've been hunting for

Carolyn Turner."

"So, what now?" I highly doubted Miss Turner would willingly hand herself over to be reaped. And I certainly didn't want to go one-on-one with her again. *Dat bitch be crazy.* Technically this was Nate's reap. No one could argue that Carolyn Turner fell under the violent criminal category. "I'll follow your lead."

"We need to talk to Samuel and get the truth about the murders."

"And how do you plan on doing that?" I seriously hoped he did not expect to use me as bait. No, no, not happening. "She's probably following him around, spying on everything he does to make sure he doesn't talk to the other women."

"Then we'll have to come up with a way to distract her." Nate stroked his chin. Though he stared at me, I could tell his mind was working on the plan. "What does Carolyn Turner love more than Samuel Parker?"

"That's easy. Herself."

"Exactly," Nate said. "All we have to do is get her to focus on herself."

We were both silent for a second, but I was already coming up with a plan. "The play. If she happened to overhear that Pammy was usurping her role as Juliet, she'd be irate and insist on commandeering the part."

"She'll be so focused on playing Juliet that she won't be thinking about Parker. That's when we'll have our little chat."

"For a few minutes at least," I said. "If Carolyn played Juliet, then we'd know exactly when and where to reap her."

"In order for this to work, we're going to need Pammy and Arlene's help." Nate straightened, giving me a hard gaze. "Are you sure you're up for this?"

"I'm fine." Even if my head felt like it was splitting in two, I would've pushed through the pain if it meant reaping Carolyn Turner's soul. My attitude might have been a little on the negative side, but attempted murder did that to me. "All right then, let's go talk to the girls. We've got a psychopath to catch."

CHAPTER EIGHT

Pushing open the door to the wardrobe room, I stuck my head inside. "Hey, how's it going?"

Arlene and Pammy looked up from their tasks. The younger ghost smiled, but Arlene simply stared over the top of her cat eyeglasses.

"It's going good," Pammy said. "We're just finishing up my gown for the death scene."

"Fantastic." Capturing the murdering ghost was for everybody's benefit, and I sincerely hoped both of the spirits saw it that way. I stopped next to the alteration table and surveyed their work. "Wow, you've been busy."

"We have something we want to ask you two," Nate said, joining the three of us. He braced his hands on top of the surface and pinned the women with a meaningful stare. "We need your help."

"Of course, I'll do whatever I can." Lowering the dark blue wad of material to her lap, Pammy gave us her undivided attention. "What is it?"

"Not so fast." Arlene set the heavy lace veil on the table and then crossed her arms over her chest. "First, tell us what you want." She waved a finger at us. "Then we'll tell you if we're going to help."

"Arlene!" The younger ghost gasped and glowered at the seamstress. "That's not very neighborly."

"Pammy, honey, trust me on this. If these two want something from us, we need to know what it is before we agree." Her gaze leveled on Nate. "What are we talking here? Snitching? Stealing?" Her eyes lit up. "Murder?"

"God no!" I pulled out the chair next to Pammy and sat, looking at her. She might be as sweet as pie and a brilliant actress, but I wasn't sure she had the same firm grasp of the obvious as Arlene did. "You know what we do, right?"

"Yes." Her face scrunched up a bit. "Well, I think I do. You help spirits cross into Heaven. That's why you can see us."

She had a knack for dumbing down a complicated situation which at the moment, I totally appreciated. "Exactly. We're grim reapers, and we originally came here to reap Mr. Parker because we were told he was bad."

"That's not true. He's a wonderful man," Pammy argued.

"We know that now." I held up my hand, cutting her off. "But we've also discovered that it's Carolyn Turner we need to reap."

"I'm in!" Arlene pushed her chair back and stood.

"Whatever you need from me, I'm in."

"But..." Pammy's gaze lingered on me, her mouth turning down in a frown. "Why do you have to reap Miss Turner?"

Time for the tough conversation. It was hard enough telling somebody that they were dead. I'd never had to reveal a spirit's murderer before. "She's done a lot of bad things." Despite the coldness I knew I'd feel, I covered her hand with mine. "She's the one that strangled you."

Again, confusion played across her face, and her mouth pulled into an even deeper frown. "No." Slowly she shook her head. "She wouldn't have done that."

"I'm afraid she did." I wish I could have made the news easier to hear, but there was no way to sugarcoat the bomb I'd just dropped. Being murdered sucked, plain and simple. Being murdered by somebody you admired sucked ten times as much. In an effort to put a positive spin on the truth, I added, "But, on a good note, it wasn't Mr. Parker as we originally thought."

"I guess that's good." Pammy shrugged. "But I always liked Miss Turner. And I thought she liked me too."

Had I ever been as young and naïve as her? A heaviness settled on my chest. My anger over the pain Carolyn Turner had caused and continued to inflict on those around her, burned through me. "It's a very good thing that it wasn't Mr. Parker." I patted her hand. "It means when he wanted you to go on as lead actress, he'd meant it. He believed in your abilities as an actress."

"Haven't I been telling you that?" Arlene took a drag off the cigarette she hadn't been holding a few minutes ago and then blew out an exaggerated stream of smoke. "And it doesn't surprise me one bit that witch was the one that did you in. She was always jealous of you. Hell, she was jealous of any woman who even looked at Mr. Parker—or walked by him—or breathed the same air." She pursed her lips and shook her head, clearly disgusted, but not surprised by our discovery. "So, what's the plan?"

"We need to make her believe that she's the one going on as Juliet tonight," Nate said. "And, we need you to keep her occupied long enough so we can talk to Parker."

"But, I thought *I* was supposed to be Juliet tonight," Pammy said.

"If everything goes as planned," I assured her, grinning. "You will. We just need to get Miss Turner out of the way first."

"Leave that to me. I know exactly what to do," Arlene said.

The determination on her face scared me a little.

She might stand five-foot-nothing, but she could be quite formidable when riled.

"What did you have in mind?" I asked.

"I've always been a behind-the-scenes kind of gal, but I'm about to give the performance of a lifetime." She turned to the young spirit. "Once she finds out Pammy is planning on playing Juliet, she'll go bat shit crazy." Arlene had obviously been picking up slang from the locals and wielded it effortlessly. "I guarantee she'll demand to go on as Juliet."

"Perfect." Nate rubbed his hands together and smiled at the seamstress. "If you can get her in here and keep her busy, we'll do the rest."

"Oh, I can get her in here. That won't be a problem. All I have to do is tell her I still have to refit Pammy's gowns." Arlene looked at the young actress. "This might be the greatest performance of your afterlife. Do you think you can go along with this plan?"

For a few seconds, Pammy stared at the pile of gowns on the table. Her eyes roved over the material, and I could tell the gravity of the situation was finally setting in. My heart went out to her, but if everything went as planned, she'd still get her night on stage. After several seconds, she looked at us and said, "Let's do it."

***

Hidden at the back of the theater near the exit door, Nate and I stood watching the empty stage. Any minute now, Arlene would begin her performance. Thankfully, we hadn't had any more encounters with the murderess which allowed us to finalize our plan. Though I wasn't fully convinced that Pammy had grasped the big picture, she was willing to do as Arlene asked and play the naïve understudy.

"Pammy!" Arlene strolled onto the stage and stopped in the center. The blue velvet gown draped limply over her one arm and the tape measure hanging around her neck were nice touches. The seamstress might have missed her calling. "Pammy, if you plan on playing Juliet tonight I need to finish altering your gown!"

"That should do it," I whispered.

"I'd be highly surprised if it took more than a few seconds for her to…" He stopped mid-sentence and grinned. "Right on cue."

Carolyn Turner materialized in front of Arlene. Even from our position, we could see that she was angry. Her spine shot ramrod straight, and she held her arms tight against her body, her hands fisted. "What are you shouting about, Arlene?"

"I'm talking about this dress." She lifted the gown and shook it. "Have you seen Pammy? I need to get these alterations finished for her performance tonight."

"She's not performing tonight. I am." Carolyn drifted closer, but to the old ghost's credit, she didn't retreat. "Like I do every year, I'm putting on my one-woman play, not Romeo and Juliet."

"That's not what Mr. Parker said." I had to hand it to Arlene, she remained cool in the face of the actresses boiling anger. "All I know is that some bigwig is coming tonight, and Mr. Parker wants to put on Romeo and Juliet to showcase everybody's talent."

"What bigwig? Why wasn't I told about this? I'm the star, not that wretched understudy." She stepped closer to the seamstress and pointed her finger at Arlene's chest. "You're going to re-alter all these dresses to fit *me*. I'll be the one going on tonight, not Pammy. Do you understand?"

"Whatever you say? You're the star." Arlene pivoted and headed offstage, but Carolyn didn't follow. Turning back, the old ghost tipped her head down and gave Carolyn her signature stare. "If you want these to fit right, you need to come with me so I can pin them." She headed offstage again, but I could hear her mumbling.

Inhaling deeply, Carolyn drew back her shoulders and glided gracefully offstage. Step one of the plan was a success, but the hardest part was still to come. Leaving our hiding spots, we bolted out of the theater and down the hall to Parker's office. After discussing the best place to speak with him, we'd decided on the sitting room where I been attacked. It wasn't my favorite place in the world, but more than likely it was his.

Though pieces of broken glass remained on the floor, the frames had been set back on the table. We filed into the room, and I closed the door behind me, sealing us in. "Mr. Parker?" I waited, but when he didn't appear after a couple of seconds, I called him again, this time a little louder. "Mr. Parker."

The temperature in the room dropped several degrees, just as it had the first time we'd been in his office. I kept my eyes riveted on the fireplace where he'd originally shown himself, hoping he would do it again.

"I'm surprised you came back."

I heard him before I saw him. And like I'd hoped, he materialized in the same spot near the fireplace. "Call me a glutton for punishment."

"You're not here to reap me, are you?" Again, he leaned his arm against the mantle as if he didn't have a care in the world. "I told you before I can't go yet."

"No," Nate said, "We're not here to reap you. We were hoping you could answer some questions for us."

"Fill in some missing information," I added. "Do you mind if we sit down? This will only take a few minutes."

"Please." He gestured toward the two leather chairs and we sat. Before claiming a spot on the slate hearth, he flipped a switch, bringing the fireplace to life. "Don't let anybody tell you that you can't be cold, or hungry, or tired, or in pain when you're a spirit. It may be a figment of my imagination, but my yearnings feel as real as when I was alive."

This was news to me, but it made sense. Otherwise, why would ghosts linger on the physical plane? I for one had no intention of hanging around. There was a beach and a margarita waiting for me in the afterlife, and I planned on soaking up the sun.

He rubbed his hands together and held them in front of the fire, before turning toward us and sitting down. "So, what can I help you with?"

Being true to form, Nate didn't pull any punches and got directly to the point. "We need to know about Carolyn Turner."

For an instant, the ghost's features tightened, the muscles in his jaw clenching and unclenching. "Can I assume you've figured out the truth?"

"We're getting there, but we'd like you to fill in some of the blanks. I know that you stop somebody from choking me." I leaned forward, resting my elbows on my thighs. "And if you hadn't, I'd probably be dead. So, first of all, thank you for that."

"You're welcome." A heavy sigh heaved from him. "I only wish I could've helped Irene, Pammy, and Evelyn."

"We were sent here to reap you because everybody thinks you murdered those three women, plus Carolyn Turner," Nate said.

"I did kill Carolyn, but not before she shot me." He pressed the palms of his hands against his eyes and spoke through gritted teeth. "I knew she wouldn't stop, so with my dying breath, I made sure she'd never kill again." He lowered his hands and looked at us. "It didn't work as you've seen firsthand. If being blamed for those murders was the price for stopping her, then I'd gladly pay it a thousand times over."

My throat tightened, this time from the conviction in his voice, not from being strangled by his crazy ex-girlfriend. Good-looking, wealthy, heroic—why did all the good ones have to be dead?

"That's what we thought," I said. "That's why we wanted to talk to you. We're hoping you can help us send Carolyn to the afterlife. The last thing we want is for her to murder again. The new owner of the theater mentioned some of the problems she had while trying to renovate."

"That was me, not Carolyn." He gave us a sheepish grin. "I was afraid somebody would get hurt, or worse, so I caused a little mischief. Nothing too serious. Just enough to shut down the work."

"That was a good idea." Nate nodded. "Evelyn's niece looks a lot like her. It would have only been a matter of time before Carolyn zeroed in on her. She would have suffered the same fate as her aunt."

"I'll do whatever I can to help." Parker held out both hands and nodded. "Anything you need, I'll make sure you get it." His piercing dark eyes softened. "It would be wonderful to have the theater open again, even if I wasn't around to enjoy it."

"If everything goes as planned," I said, "we'll make sure you never have to worry about Miss Turner or the theater again." I would've held out my hand to shake on our deal, but I'd had quite enough ghost contact for one night—I didn't care how handsome he was. "I'd say at the very least you deserve that."

"Thank you." The tension eased from his shoulders and he gave us a smile that would've made any female's heart flutter. "I know it's crazy, but I feel partially responsible for what Carolyn has done."

"Don't," Nate said, his tone abrupt. "It's not your fault your girlfriend turned out to be a psychopathic killer."

Please, Nate, tell us how you really feel. The vehemence in his voice made me wonder if a crazy girlfriend—or two—lingered in his past. I made a mental note to ask him about it. He called it prying, while I called it being a caring partner. Maybe it was Willow from the Grim Reaper Services payroll department. There seemed to be something between them, though I couldn't tell whether it was hostility or sexual tension. I kind of hoped it was the first option.

"I know you're right, but none of those women would've been murdered if it hadn't been for her unhealthy infatuation with me." His image wavered, growing more solid the longer he sat in front of us. "Even though I was unsuccessful once in stopping her, and I paid for that with my life—" He shook his head. "—I have nothing left to lose." His smile returned. "And everything to gain."

"First off, we need you to announce to Carolyn that

tonight you'll be putting on Shakespeare's Romeo and Juliet, and casting Pammy in the lead," I said. "We've already had Arlene put the bug in her ear, and you confirming it will really get her riled up."

Samuel flinched. "You're trying to make her angry?"

"Our goal is to keep her so focused on playing Juliet that she misses what's going on around her."

"What about Pammy?" Parker asked. "I'd hate to disappoint her again."

"She and Arlene are in on the plan as well. And, if everything goes smoothly," Nate said, "Pammy will still get her time in the spotlight."

"Then count me in." Samuel stood. "I'll go make the announcement now."

We both rose and followed him to the door. "Things are about to get interesting," I said. "And I want a front-row seat."

We now had everybody we needed on board, and even though this was Nate's reap, the plan was going to take a village—or in this case, the cast and crew.

CHAPTER NINE

The shrill nagging voice of Carolyn seeped through the fitting room door. It seemed she was every bit the diva the ghosts had said she was. "I can't believe Samuel would do this without my permission. What was he thinking casting Pammy as Juliet? Clearly, I'm the best Juliet."

"Maybe he wanted a fresh face," Arlene said in a deadpan voice. "You know, somebody who doesn't bitch so much."

"You'd better watch it, Arlene, I can make your life very miserable."

"That ship sailed a long time ago, Carolyn."

"Ouch!" A high-pitched squeak yipped from the diva. "You stuck me with that pin on purpose."

"Did I? Then I suggest you hold still."

Samuel brushed past us and braced his hand against the door. "Time for my big scene," he whispered.

Nate and I stepped to the right so we wouldn't be seen. I held my breath, anticipation jetting through me. It was like being inside our own reality TV show, except all the players were dead, besides Nate and me.

"It's about time you showed up." Carolyn's voice reverberated down the hall. I could only imagine what she'd been like when she was alive. Probably twice as possessive and arrogant. "I've taken the liberty of recasting Juliet. I will be playing the part."

"It's a pretty complicated role," he said. "I don't think you can handle it."

"Of course, I can handle it, you idiot!" Something smashed against the wall beside the door. We both leaped back in an effort to avoid projectile shards of white porcelain. "I'm the *only* one who can handle this role."

"What do you say about this, Pammy?"

"Yes, Pammy, what do you think about me—the obvious choice—playing Juliet?" Carolyn echoed.

The room was silent for a few seconds, drawing out the tension. I didn't know if Pammy was truly afraid to speak, or if she was plying her craft to the current situation. Finally, she said, "Of course Miss Turner should play Juliet. She's much more talented than I am and has the savoir faire the role requires."

"See, what did I tell you? Even Pammy knows I have the savor…the savoy…that savvy thing she just said."

Samuel let her comment hang in the air, not responding immediately. Though we couldn't see exactly what was going on, I could imagine his cool expression and Carolyn's pissed off glower. At some point, he'd need to close the door so we could get things ready for the rest of the plan, but I think he hadn't just so we could enjoy the scene.

After an extended hesitation, he said, "All right, Carolyn, but first I want you to do a run through of a couple of scenes. If I like what I see, you can play Juliet. But if I don't, Pammy gets the part."

"You're making me audition?" A loud crashing came from inside the room. It sounded as if she'd overturned a table. "Are you kidding me?"

"Take it or leave it," Samuel said. "That's my condition."

Turning my head toward Nate, I mimicked an open-mouth laugh. Nothing gave me more satisfaction than hearing the snooty hag get her comeuppance. The psychopath had tried to kill me. He grinned back, clearly enjoying the drama as much as I was.

"Fine," Carolyn quipped, "But I choose the scenes."

"No, I want to see the death scene, after you see Romeo drink the poison and die. Start there. I want to hear your final speech." Samuel stepped back across the threshold but continued to stare into the room. His gaze didn't wander to us or give any indication that we were mere inches away. "You may decide on the second scene.

Finish up with your wardrobe alterations. I'll expect you on stage fully costumed, in an hour."

Not waiting for her to agree or disagree, he closed the door and faced us. Again, a crash sounded against the wall. If we didn't get her reaped soon there wouldn't be another coffee cup, statue, or anything breakable left in the place. Samuel flicked his head toward the end of the hall and we crept past the fitting room door, stopping at the end.

"That should do it," he said.

"You were awesome." Unable to resist, I rubbed his shoulder. "I think you missed your calling as an actor."

"I was always more of a behind-the-scenes man. That's where I do my best work."

I bet he did.

"We need to get ready for the next stage." Nate gripped my upper arm and pulled me toward the theater. "This could get a little tricky."

***

An hour later I found myself ensconced behind one of the backstage curtains. Besides Samuel, who sat in the front row, the theater was empty. All ushers and early arriving patrons had been cleared, much to their chagrin.

Now Carolyn stood on a makeshift balcony, spouting the most famous lines from Romeo and Juliet.

"Romeo, Romeo, wherefore art thou Romeo?" I peered at her through a tiny slit in the curtains. Her hands gestured wildly in front of her, as if in the throes of an epileptic seizure. "Deny it no farther and refuse my name."

"Deny thy father and refuse thy name." Samuel's voice rose to just below a yell, the irritation apparent in the way he enunciated each word. "Not deny it no farther and refuse my name."

"Yeah, yeah, I got it." She flipped her hands at him, gesturing for him to be quiet. I bit my lip in an effort not to laugh. Wow, she stunk. Talk about getting by on your looks. That had to be the case because she had no talent whatsoever. "Deny my father and refuse thy name," she said in a robotic voice.

Listening to her massacre the lines was torturous, and that was saying a lot coming from a grim reaper. I'd been attacked by demons, dragged across the tundra by the ghost of a moose, had the spirit of an evil vampire try to possess my body, and yet all of those were preferable than having to listen to Carolyn Turner act her way through Romeo and Juliet.

"Stop!" Samuel stood and shook his head. "I've

heard enough."

"Wait!" She turned and disappeared through the facade's door. Even though she was a ghost, I could hear her footsteps thundering down the wooden stairs behind the scene. It was as if she thought she was still alive. Again, I didn't know if Halloween could be the reason, but she wasn't the only spirit who had solidified and moved like a corporeal being. A few seconds later, she shot through the downstairs door. "I still have a death scene to do." She propped her fists on her hips, looking like she belonged in The Taming of the Shrew instead of Romeo and Juliet. "You promised."

I shifted to get a glimpse of the theater owner. Boy, the guy played a convincing part. He released an exaggerated exhale. "Fine, but only because I keep my word. Go change into your death scene costume."

"I don't need to change." She indicated the blue and gold gown she currently wore. "I'll just wear this to do the scene."

"Part of being Juliet is the ability to proficiently work with the wardrobe. Much of the scene is spent laying down, or maneuvering a dying Romeo onto your lap." He lowered himself back to the chair." I need to know you can do this without fumbling around."

She jerked her fists off her hips, directing them toward the floor, and stamped her foot. Though she didn't actually argue with him, she did give a loud guttural growl of exasperation before stomping offstage.

When I knew for sure she was gone, I stepped out from behind the curtain. Samuel stood and jogged up the steps to join me, and together we pushed the makeshift deathbed to the center of the stage.

"Okay," he said. "Let's get Nate in place."

A second later my partner strolled out from behind the opposite curtain. It took all of my willpower to maintain my professional bearing and not laugh and point. He was dressed head to toe in Shakespearean garb, which included a pair of beige wool tights. Thank God for that tunic thing covering his junk, because the tights left little to the imagination. Sure, I might've had the odd fantasy about Nate and what he looked like naked, but there was a time and place for that kind of stuff, and this was not that time, nor the place.

His eyes skated to me, held for a second as if daring me to say anything, and then cut back to the bed. "Where do you want me?"

"Climb up here and lay on your side." Nate did as he asked. Samuel moved forward and shifted Nate's body, adjusting the placement of his legs and arms. "We don't want her to see your face, so keep your arm draped across your head like this."

"Yeah, that should work," Nate said. After making a few adjustments, I couldn't even tell it was my partner. "So, I just lay here? I don't have to say anything?"

Samuel shook his head. "No, I'll have her pick up the scene after Romeo has died."

"And I'll wait over here." I pointed toward the curtain I'd been hiding behind. "In case you need help."

"Thanks, Carron," Nate said from under his arm.

I smiled, unsure whether he was thanking me for having his back, or for not teasing him about the tights. "That's what partners are for."

I made it to my hiding spot mere seconds before Carolyn came stomping back on stage. "What's this?" She glared at Nate laying on the bed and then at Samuel in the audience. "Where's Mikey?"

"He's getting ready. This is his understudy." Samuel folded his hands over his stomach and crossed his legs, giving her a bored expression. "Can we begin, please? Despite your need to claim all my attention, I do have other matters to take care of."

"This is so unprofessional," she grumbled, taking

her place on the far side of the bed. "Is he going to say any lines?"

"No, just pick it up from the happy dagger line."

Carolyn started in on what I could only assume was her rendition of the death scene. I don't know what version of Shakespeare she'd learned, but it certainly wasn't the same one I'd read in high school. Or that anyone else had ever read for that matter. As I watched her fumble through the scene, it was hard for me to believe that this had been the same ghost who had nearly strangled me. She was so inept and clumsy.

Still, I'd seen death do weird things to spirits. One minute they were calm, and the next they morphed into a violent specter. She wasn't right in the head when she was alive. No telling how that psychosis translated in death.

When she reached for Nate, I tensed, my heart beating faster. It took a couple of fumbling tries, but Carolyn finally managed to lift him into her arms. Stepping from behind the curtain, I inched toward them. Samuel remained unmoving in the front row. His eyes darting from me and back to the deathbed was the only hint that he knew I was there. He shifted, sitting straighter—more alert.

Though from my spot behind Carolyn I couldn't see what was going on, I knew the second Nate enacted his *intent* and claimed her to be reaped.

"What are you doing?" She pushed away from Nate, but couldn't loosen his hold. That was one of the perks of a grim reaper's intent—and also one of the dangers. "Let go of me."

She stumbled backward, pulling him off the table with her. They barreled toward me. Her once solid body now grew translucent and gauzy. No doubt she would try to flee or evaporate. They always did. The soft leather boots Nate wore had no traction, and as Carolyn attempted her escape, she dragged him along with her. I, on the other hand, had dressed for the part. Digging in the heels of my hiking boots, I braced for impact.

They hit me with the power of a speeding truck. Even though I was able to grab on to Carolyn, the force knocked the breath out of me. I gasped for air but clung tight to the spirit as she levitated.

Our bodies lifted off the ground, my toes barely grazing the stage floor. Screams poured from Carolyn as she tried to break free of our hold. Glancing up, I jerked backward, almost releasing her at the sight of her skeletal face. There was no arguing that the woman had a lot of pent-up rage.

Arms encircled my waist pulling the three of us to

the floor. Samuel, now almost fully corporeal, added his weight to the pile. "It's over! No more, Carolyn," he said. "No more killing."

She stopped thrashing and growled at him. "You don't tell me when it's over. I say when it's over." A maniacal laugh erupted from her. "And it will never be over, Samuel. As long as there is a breath in this body, I will take everything from you."

Still pinning her legs to the floor, he sat back on his haunches and stared down at his onetime girlfriend. "You already have, Carolyn. You've taken everything that mattered to me, but I'm going to make sure you can't do that to anyone else ever again."

He bent and grabbed her by the puffy sleeves. She flailed and kicked against his hold, screeching for us to let her go. It took our combined effort, but we managed to wrangle her to her feet.

"Pick!" Nate yelled for his porter.

It only took a couple of seconds for the blue light to appear, elongate, and widened to the shape of a door. The rectangle slid open to reveal an elevator, and standing inside, Nate's porter, Pick. With his slick pinstripe suit and the tiny bumps on his head that reminded me of horns, he was creepy with a capital C.

"Nate, what goodies have you brought for me today?" His gaze tracked over Carolyn, and I swear he licked his lips.

"I am so glad it's you going into the elevator and not me," I whispered into her ear.

Her head twisted in an unnatural angle to look at me. "We'll just see about that."

"This is Carolyn Turner," Nate informed his porter. We inched closer to the elevator. "I have no doubt she is on your list."

"Ahh, yes, the murderess." Again, Pick's black gaze moved over the ghost and I swore I physically felt it. "It must be my lucky day."

Unlike my porter's elevator, Pick's always glowed red inside, as if the fires of Hell were illuminating it from the bottom up. And on that note, it would be a frigid day in Hell before I stepped foot in Pick's elevator. Not going to happen—ever.

I don't know what kind of supercharged ecto-mojo Carolyn Turner had stored up, but one minute we were moving her toward the elevator, and the next the three of us were flying through the air. I landed hard on the wooden floor and skidded to a stop inches from the elevator to Hell. Spots clouded my vision, and when it cleared, I found myself staring up into Pick's black orbs. I lay there, paralyzed with the thought that he might actually drag me inside.

"She's getting away." The porter bent, bringing his face even closer to mine, and said in a low smooth, menacing voice. "It's best we don't let that happen, Ms. Carron."

"Right." Scrambling like a crab, I put as much distance as I could between the elevator and me, and then jumped to my feet, evaluating the scene in the split-second.

Both Nate and Samuel seem dazed but unhurt. Maniacal laughter split the air and rang through the theater as the psychotic ghost swooped out over the seats and around the balconies. We'd never catch her now. She knew who we were and why we were there. But the thought of leaving her free to rain death and destruction was unthinkable.

I crept to the edge of the stage, watching her zoom around the interior of the theater. Though I unhooked the scythe from my belt, I kept the cylinder latched. She'd tried to kill me once, and I wanted to see if I could get her to do it again.

"That had to be the worst Juliet I've ever heard!" My comment didn't even cause her manic flight pattern to slow. "You suck as an actress!" And just to add insult to injury, I shouted, "And Samuel likes me better than you!" I jabbed a finger at her like I'd seen those angry girls on the web do. "That's right." I circled my head and snapped my fingers. "We're going to live happily ever after together, because I'm all that, and you are nothing but a dried-up bag of bones. And..." I continued, really getting into it now, "I am a much better kisser than you are. So why would he want you when he can have all of—" I stroked my hands down the front of my body. "—This!"

She hovered forty feet above me in the center of the theater. Her chin dipped, and her eyes pinned me with a look filled with so much hatred I could physically feel it prickle against my skin.

"Yeah, that did it," Nate said from behind me. "I hope you have a plan."

"It's time to pull out the big gun, boys." I braced myself, but sent up a quick prayer that she wouldn't plow into me again. "This is going to get ugly."

"Though I agree wholeheartedly that you're all that, I question whether you know what you're doing," Samuel said in an unsure voice. "I've never seen her this angry."

"Don't worry, I have that effect on people." I grinned. "And Sam?"

"Yeah?"

"Thanks for thinking I'm all that."

He laughed. "You're welcome."

A shrill shriek exploded from Carolyn. I almost had to cover my ears against the splitting scream but managed to remain where I was, fixed and focused. As I knew she would, the spirit swooped toward me with her arms extended, and her hands ready to reclaim my neck. Though she came at me like a bullet, I forced myself to wait until she was a few yards away before releasing my scythe.

The handle hissed and lengthened, and the smoky blade swirled up and out, forming to a sharp gleaming point an instant later. I darted to the side, narrowly avoiding her hands, and brought my weapon down in an arc. The scythe's blade sliced through Carolyn, splitting her in two. One second she was there, the next the air was empty.

That's the thing about my sweet scythe, no porter required. Reaping with the weapon was clean and efficient, even if it was rather impersonal. In this case, though, I was okay with that.

"Nice one, Carron," Nate said.

"Thanks." I pivoted and smiled, holding up my hand. "I think that deserves a high-five."

At first, Nate just stared at my hand and then at my

face. I waited. I knew he wouldn't let me down. I'd just pulled off some serious ninja reaping. He totally owed me five. After a few seconds, he sighed.

"What the hell?" He leveled a solid slap against my hand. "You deserve it."

I grabbed him by the shoulders and shook him. "We deserve it, partner."

"That was amazing," Samuel said. He held up his hand, and I slapped the crap out of it. Now there was a man who knew how to high-five a sista. "I've never seen anything like that before."

"Don't let this hockey-mom face fool you." I twisted the ornate ring at the top of the handle, and my scythe slid back into its cylinder. "I'm a badass when I have to be."

"I see that." Samuel's gaze skated over me in a way that seriously had me questioning how long he'd remain corporeal. "I think your agency is lucky to have you—both of you."

"Ms. Carron," Pick called from the entrance of the elevator. "Though you are quite a sight to watch, you do take all the fun out of reaping."

"Uhhh, sorry?" *So not sorry.* He tipped his head toward me and winked as the door closed and then disappeared. I frowned and turned to Nate. "Did he just wink at me?"

"I think he likes you."

"God forbid." I shuddered. Making friends with Pick was right up there with petting a cobra. One second you're both swaying to the music, and the next he's latched on and is pulling you into the bowels of Hell. "He makes Hal seem tame."

"Tame is not a word I would use for your grandfather."

I held up my finger. "Grandfather is a word I wouldn't use to describe my grandfather."

"Good point," he agreed.

"You two are quite the couple." Samuel's gaze squinted at us. "I have no idea what you're talking about and yet I find you completely entertaining."

"Speaking of entertaining…" I held my arms out wide. "It's show time?"

Carolyn was gone, which meant my chances for surviving the night had skyrocketed from around thirty percent to nearly a hundred. It was a job well done, but the night wasn't over yet. We had a play to attend. And if Evelyn Git was half as good as she said she was, we had hundreds of ghosts to help crossover. It was going to be a busy night.

CHAPTER TEN

The house filled to capacity and a buzz of excitement hummed through the theater. I'd heard whispers about this being the first real play in decades. The patrons had dressed to the nines in suits, tuxedos, gowns, and party dresses. There was enough bling in the theater tonight to fund a dozen renovation projects.

I claimed a couple of VIP seats in the balcony; after all, this play wouldn't have happened if it hadn't been for us. I hefted my two-pound bag of candy onto my lap and got comfortable.

"This is going to be great." Evelyn Git emerged from the ether onto the chair next to me. "I couldn't be happier with the turnout."

"Is this all your doing?" I unwrapped a mini chocolate-peanut bar and popped it in my mouth.

"This is what I do—did." She held out her arms like Moses at the Red Sea. "Behold, the power of public relations."

"Impressive," I said around a mouthful of chocolate. "You should get a job at GRS. They could use somebody like you."

"Maybe I'll have a chat with the powers to be and

see what we can come up with." She slapped her legs. "Well, no rest for the wicked. I've got more schmoozing to do."

"Knock 'em dead." I snorted, laughing at my own joke.

In a blink of an eye, she disappeared. I'd been kidding about her working at GRS, but I'd seen crazier things than that happen since I'd become a grim reaper. In this line of work, anything was possible.

Nate pulled aside the curtain and slid onto the chair next to me. "Great seats."

"Only the best." I held out the bag of Halloween candy to him. "Treat?"

He leaned toward me and scanned the options. After a few seconds, he lifted his head and smiled. "No, thank you."

"Come on." I rattled the bag. "You have got to be hungry after the night we've had. It's Halloween." I shoved the candy toward him. "Just one piece in honor of a job well done."

"Fine, but only one." Reaching over, he grabbed the first piece his hand touched and then tucked it into his jacket pocket. I knew he wouldn't eat it. "This isn't going to become a thing, is it?"

"I don't know," I said, pulling the foil wrapper off the chocolate, giving him a pointed stare. "It might become a Halloween thing."

I tossed the candy into my mouth and turned my attention to the theater floor. His stare brushed against the side of my face like butterfly wings, and it took all my willpower not to glance at him again.

Times like these were dangerous. The case solved, the client reaped, Nate sitting very close—it was enough to test any girl's self-control. I really needed to start dating. This schoolgirl crush was getting me nowhere.

"Look." I pointed to the far side of the theater. "There's Ginger."

The cigarette-girl drifted along the outer row, the tray hanging around her neck. She called out her wares, stopping periodically to sell one of her items. As my gaze tracked around the lower level, I recognized several ghosts—a couple of the patrons speaking with Evelyn, the ushers, and the little irritating guy that looked like a ferret. They'd all become familiar in such a short time, and I wondered if we'd bump into each other again in the afterlife. For someone who worked in the death/afterlife field, I sure didn't know much about what went on once a spirit was delivered to their destination. And to be honest, I was in no hurry to find out.

The lights dimmed, and the spotlight illuminated the stage. This was it, Pammy's big night. I sat on the edge of my seat, waiting for her to make her first appearance. It took a while, but the Capulet-Montague brawl sufficiently entertained me until then.

When she walked onto the stage, I reached over and grabbed Nate's hand. It just happened. Seeing her take command of the performance made me feel like a proud mother—well—maybe older sister—and I could barely contain my excitement for her.

It took a few seconds for me to realize Nate hadn't released my hand, and in fact, his thumb rubbed back and forth over mine. I swallowed hard but kept my eyes on the performance. It would be too weird if I looked at him, or in any way acknowledged our connection. And I wasn't quite sure how I'd retrieve my hand from him—not that I wanted to—except, eventually I'd want to eat more candy.

That turned out not to be a problem when a few minutes later Samuel joined us in the balcony VIP section. "I knew she'd be wonderful," he whispered. His gaze remained riveted on Pammy, and a contented peaceful smile curved his mouth. "She's the real deal."

"You have an eye for talent," Nate said. His hand

slipped from mine.

"Yeah, she's amazing." I set the Halloween candy on the floor, and locked my fingers together, settling my hands on my lap. Maybe this would prevent me from reaching for Nate during a particularly emotional part of the play. "And this is a real treat for us. Once a client is reaped, we don't have much of a chance to socialize."

"Thank you again. I can finally rest in peace, as they say." His smile set off an eruption of tiny butterflies in my stomach. He was a handsome man and would no doubt be a hit in the afterlife. "As can a few others, I think."

"We're happy to help anybody who wants to cross over, including you," Nate said a little too enthusiastically.

Okay, nothing like making the client feel unwanted. I slowly turned my head and gave him a questioning glower. He returned my scowl. I had to wonder if he might be a tiny bit jealous. A girl could hope.

We turned our attention back to the play, and soon the performers had whisked me away to the world of the Capulets and Montagues.

Pammy was fabulous, but I couldn't help feel a little sad for her. Her death had been senseless, the result of a sick and jealous mind. At least she'd gotten one night to put on the performance of a lifetime.

As the final curtain fell, the audience erupted in a standing ovation, which lasted for several minutes. We made our way down to the stage, and as Pammy took her final bow, Samuel Parker presented her with a bouquet of roses that befitted any Broadway star.

I blinked back the tingle of tears threatening to form and inhaled deeply. This had been quite a night. Most of the time we just went one-on-one with our spirits, sending them to their designated destination. But tonight, I felt like I would be saying goodbye to actual friends.

After the applause died down, Samuel took center stage, announcing that anyone wishing to join him in the next act would be welcome.

When the entire theater broke into applause again, Nate leaned in and said, "I think we're going to need a little help."

"I'll call Constantine." I ducked offstage and down to the break room where I'd left my bag.

He answered on the first ring. "I've got people on the way, Carron. Nice work."

Before I'd even said a word, he hung up. "Okay, good talk," I mumbled into the mouthpiece. After clicking off the phone, I shoved it into my back pocket.

"I want to thank you again."

I spun to see Samuel standing just inside the door. He walked toward me, his body looking as physical as mine, and stopped a fraction inside my personal bubble. This time though, I didn't really mind. "You're quite welcome." He was good-looking, like billionaire bad boy good-looking, except nice. "Just doing my job."

He lifted his hand and caressed my cheek. Unlike before, his touch was only cool, not a painful chill. "I want you to promise me something." He didn't wait for me to ask what it was. "When you get to the other side, I want you to look me up."

I didn't even know if that was possible. Did reapers even go to the same place as normal people, or did we had a special afterlife? But I was game for giving it a try. "I promise."

I think he was going to kiss me, as was evident by the slight bend in his posture, but Nate interrupted us. "The others are here."

"Great." My eyes searched Samuel's face, and I smiled. C'est la vie, this was not meant to be. I stepped back. "We could use your help."

"I'm all yours," Samuel said, winking at me.

A wistful sigh slipped from me. Why were all the good one's dead?

With that, he turned and glided out the door, his body growing more translucent. Nate waited until the spirit was gone before turning back to me. "Did I interrupt something?"

Was that jealousy I detected? I gave him my sweetest smile. "Nope. You weren't interrupting a thing."

"Are you sure, because it looked like you two were having a moment."

"Oh, I forgot to tell you." I brushed past him and headed down the hall. "I took a picture of you in those tights."

"You better not have." He followed me down the hall. "Carron, let me see your phone."

"Nope." I picked up my pace. "Don't worry, I won't show anybody. It will be strictly for my personal enjoyment."

"Not if I have anything to say about it."

Bolting down the hall, I made it all the way to the stage before he got a hold of my phone. I didn't really have a picture, unfortunately.

Even with five other reapers and their porters, it took us another two hours to empty the theater. Most spirits had happily jumped on any open elevator, intent on continuing the party on the ethereal plane. Pammy and

Arlene were two of the last spirits to leave. After saying our goodbyes and well wishes, I loaded them onto Hal's elevator.

Tonight, he was dressed in black and orange satin. It took a lot of discipline to not comment on the fact that he reminded me of a gigantic jack o'lantern. I'd describe his style as anything over the top.

"Who makes your clothes?" Arlene asked. She fingered the fabric at his sleeve. "They're nice. Not everybody could wear this color." She lowered her hand and peered over her glasses at him, which was kind of funny because it was the exact same expression he was giving her. "Have you ever considered fringe?"

"Madam, you are a woman after my own heart." Hal turned to me and smiled. "Liiiiisa…" He always dragged my name out, making it three syllables longer than it actually was. "You always bring me the most interesting people."

"Well Hal, I live to please." I gave a little wave. "Going up?"

"Wait for me!" Evelyn Git tromped up the steps and jogged to the elevator. She stopped beside me, her breath coming out in pants as if breathing was still a required function. "Whew, I thought I missed my ride. Listen, tell my niece that I'm thrilled she is taking over the theater, and she has my blessings to move forward with the renovations."

"I'm sure she'll be thrilled to know that," I said.

She flicked her head in Nate's direction. Thankfully he was too far away to hear. "And tell her not to let that one over there get away. He's got it all if you know what I mean. Prime choice."

"All righty, then." I wasn't about to tell Lizzy Git any such thing. I pushed Evelyn into the elevator. "Have a great trip."

A chorus of goodbyes filtered through the doors as they closed and then silenced. I pressed my hands to my lower back and stretched. The siren's call of my bed was growing stronger, and exhaustion was taking hold. I walked to where Nate and Samuel stood. The only elevator left was Pick's.

"I guess I'm the last one." Samuel eyed the interior. "Is this a one-way trip down?"

"To be honest," Nate said, "I don't know."

"Wait." My gaze bounced between Nate and Pick. "He's not going to Hell, is he?"

"Sorry, Carron, but he killed Carolyn Turner," Nate said.

"In self-defense," I argued.

"It's not our call." Nate shrugged. "I don't think it's fair either, but we have to have faith that the powers to be will be reasonable."

"Listen," Samuel said, "Like I told you before, I would have paid any price a thousand times over to have stopped Carolyn. If my fate is to go to Hell, then I except it." He smirked. "I pray it's not my fate. I mean, I'm not stupid. So, maybe you could say a little prayer for me."

"I will, Samuel." Anger over the injustice poured through me. "I'm going to say a thousand prayers for you. And don't you worry, I know people."

And by people, I meant beings on the other side. As a matter of fact, one of my good friends was a demon. I bet if I asked her, she'd make sure Samuel got a fair shake.

"Thank you, Lisa. That means a lot to me." He stepped into the elevator and turned toward us. "Here's to the next act."

As the elevator door slid closed I said, "Break a leg."

Nate and I eased away as the elevator pulled into a tight blue line, shrunk, and then winked out of sight. Silence blanketed the theater. It was just the two of us now. I lifted my wrist and tapped on my fitness tracker. It was nearly five o'clock and seeing the time suddenly made me all the more tired.

"Well, I guess we're done here." Despite the fact that he'd been up nearly twenty-four hours, nearly thrown through the wall, and tossed to the ground by a psychotic ghost, he seemed as fresh as he did when we first arrived at the theater. It was so unfair. "Let's get our stuff from the break room—" He paused. "—and then I'll buy you breakfast."

"Is this a ploy to try to steal my phone?" I smirked. "Because I don't really have a picture of you." I was such a pushover, spilling my guts with the least provocation.

"No, that's not why I asked." He stepped so far inside my personal zone I had to crane my neck to look at him. His gaze held mine. He reached up and took hold of the edges of my jacket. "I asked because I want to have breakfast with you."

This felt like a moment—like the kind I'd been hoping for. He'd initiated the closeness, but now I wasn't sure what to do. Where should I put my hands? Did I slip them inside his pockets or wrap them around his waist? I ended up hooking my fingers onto his belt loops.

"You want to have breakfast with me? No ulterior motives."

"Oh." His eyes narrowed. "I definitely have ulterior motives, but for now I'll settle for breakfast."

"You don't mean that Spam in the break room, do you?"

"Not unless you'd rather have that."

"Breakfast at a restaurant is good. I like breakfast."

We were definitely having a moment. My heart raced, and I finally gave into the urge to lean into him. "Nate?"

"Yes, Lisa?"

Were you planning on kissing me?"

A smile tugged at his lips. "Yes, Lisa."

"Now?"

In answer, he lowered his head and slanted his mouth over mine. I couldn't have stopped myself if I'd wanted to. I wound my arms around his neck and pulled him closer. Thankfully the guilt I thought I'd feel over kissing another man besides my dead husband never surfaced.

Maybe because it was Nate. He was more than just another guy. Or maybe it was the soft way he claimed my mouth, and how his right arm crept its way around my lower back and drew me to him. There were probably a lot of reasons, but at the moment I was having a hard time concentrating on anything but his lips.

We broke off our kiss and eased away from each other, otherwise, we probably would have never made it out of the theater. "Okay then." I picked up my bag, slung it over my shoulder, and then looked at him. "Where should we eat?"

I'd just had one of the most amazing nights of my life. I'd ninja chopped a serial killer with my scythe, helped hundreds of souls cross over, made new friends, and possibly landed myself a boyfriend.

Happy Halloween to me.

Want more holiday fun? Don't miss Dead Jolly.

DEAD JOLLY

A GRIM REALITY NOVELLA

The holidays are here, and I'm up to my eyeballs in Christmas spirit—or should I say "spirits". Life is like that now that I'm a grim reaper.

My holidays get an extra helping of festive weirdness when the Casanova of mall Santas kicks the bucket. Instead of crossing over, he sets out to spread his own special brand of Christmas magic to a number of single ladies in town.

I'll admit, as a widow I'm hesitant to stop him from gifting his Christmas miracle, but as a reaper, it's my job to pack his yule log and jingle bells off to the netherworld.

After all, everybody knows Santa is only supposed to come once a year.

Or find out how it all started in To Catch Her Death.

TO CATCH HER DEATH
BOOK 1

What do you get when you cross a hockey mom with the grim reaper?

Me, Lisa Carron.

If being a depressed, frumpy, widowed mother of three wasn't bad enough, I just found out I'm a grim reaper. I know what you're thinking. *Wow, that's kind of sexy and full of awesomeness.* Hardly. Oh, and my clients? Stupid people. Like I don't get enough of that from the living.

Since Alaska is big and angels of death are few, I've been partnered with reaper extraordinaire, Nate Cramer. He's strong, silent, and way too good looking for my recently widowed state. Oh, and he reaps violent criminals, so that should be interesting. Forget the danger and the hours of self-analysis it will take for me to find my reaper mojo. My biggest problem? Hiding it all from my overly attentive family and nosy neighbors.

Now that's going to take a miracle.

STYX & STONED
BOOK 2

Las Vegas! All expenses paid!

Normally, a trip like that would be a dream come true for a widowed, mother of three, who just happens to be grim reaper. Here's the thing though, situations rarely work out as I imagine they should. And usually not in my favor.

This time isn't any different. Instead of the endless free drinks and gambling I'd been hoping for, I get the opposite—demons, water zombies, and a bimbo ghost roommate, who gives new meaning to the phrase dead drunk.

But it's not all bad. I'm making new friends, learning

spectacular reaper skills, and saving souls. I just hope I don't lose mine before I can get the Underworld all sorted out.

A Note from Boone

Thank you for choosing Dead Spooky. I truly hope you enjoyed it.

Every time a reader tells me they love my books I'm humbled and thrilled. Their satisfaction means I've done my job as a writer. My readers are the reason I stumble to my office every morning with coffee in hand and create new worlds and characters. So, thank you again for being my motivation to continue doing what I love.

Boone

About the Author

Boone is a *USA Today* Bestselling Author with dozens of titles under her belt, ranging from romantic comedy to medieval fantasy. With a particular love for all things paranormal, Boone weaves the strange and quirky into her books, and is especially drawn to stories about the afterlife.

She lives in the beautiful state of Alaska with her husband and twin daughters and truly believes with her mad survival skills she would rock a zombie apocalypse.

Printed in Great Britain
by Amazon